RETURN TO
ATALAN

By

Richard Brewin

Chapter 1

Isla took a sip of her lemonade as she lay on a beach towel enjoying the afternoon sun whilst generic pop music blasted out of her phone's speaker. Unfortunately for her, she wasn't on a beach somewhere listening to the sea crashing against the rocks but instead sunbathing in her back garden. Apart from the singing of the birds, the only sound she could hear was that of the traffic from a nearby road.

"Isla," called her mum from the kitchen.

"Yeah," replied Isla, without even turning her head to look at where the voice had come from.

"I've got a conference call for the next few hours so I will be in the office. If you want a snack, help yourself," shouted her mum through the open kitchen window.

"Ok," answered Isla. She was far more interested in selecting another similar sounding pop song and checking to see if any of her friends were online than paying much attention to her mum.

It was the start of the summer holidays, and Isla was already a little bit bored. Many of her friends had already gone away for their summer breaks or were in holiday clubs run by her school. Isla was currently at home with her parents as both of their jobs allowed them to work from here.

Today her mum was at home while her dad had left early to go to a meeting somewhere. He had told Isla where he was going, but like many 11-year-olds, she hadn't paid much attention.

In a few days, Isla would be going to her grandma's to spend a week there as she did every summer, and then she would be getting on a plane and jetting off to some unpronounceable Spanish resort for the James family holiday that she was very excited about. Her holidays with her parents were always great fun, and she had many fond memories of previous trips away.

As Isla lay on the beach towel humming away to one of her favourite songs, she thought back to her last trip to her grandma's during the school holidays. It had been just over a year since she had found the magical book which had transported her to the far off land of Atalan for the adventure of a lifetime. Most days, she would think back to her time spent with Oliver and Fartybubble, the two Unkerdunkies who had helped her in her quest to get back home. She really missed those two along with Fizzbit the troll and Wally the wizard and often wondered what they were up to now.

On her return to Earth, she had decided not to tell her grandma or her parents about her Atalan adventures and had kept it a secret from everyone except her best friend Ellie, who she had made pinkie swear that she would never tell a soul about it.

4

Isla had asked her grandma if she could keep the book she had found in the bric-a-brac box, and it was now stood on her shelf in her bedroom, the lock safely fastened, and the ornate goblin key stashed away in her jewellery box. At times, Isla had contemplated opening the book, but the thought of getting stranded back on Atalan and away from her family was enough to mean that the book had remained shut to this day. She had the book, she had her memories, and she even had a video on her phone of a pair of buzzagons flying through the sky to remind her of her time there.

As Isla sunbathed in the privacy of her garden, she heard a rustling coming from the bushes at the bottom of the lawn. At first, she thought it was just birds, as they often had sparrows and robins in the garden, but as she listened, the rustling grew louder, and whatever was causing it sounded much larger than a bird. Maybe a squirrel, she thought as she sat up to take a better look.

As she did so, she noticed the leaves that had fallen from the trees and had covered the bottom of the garden were now being whipped up into the air and were swirling around, almost as if a mini typhoon was blowing through. How strange, Isla thought since there wasn't a cloud in the sky, and she couldn't feel any breeze herself. As she continued to watch, she noticed a white light appear. At first, it was only small as if the sun's rays were bouncing off a hidden mirror somewhere, but then the light started to get bigger and bigger and bigger until it engulfed the entire bottom half of the garden.

Isla grabbed her phone and got to her feet; she wasn't sure what was going on, but whatever it was, it was starting to freak her out. Just then, the bright light disappeared, and there stood at the bottom of Isla's garden was a man who she had never seen before in her life.

Isla's first instinct was to scream, but before she could make a sound, the stranger spoke to her.

"Are you Isla?" asked the man in a soft and gentle voice.

The fact he knew her name made Isla stop in her tracks. Who was this man, and where had he come from? There was no way through the dense bushes that formed a boundary to the garden that lay behind. Surely, there must be a logical explanation, Isla thought. He couldn't have just come out of thin air, could he?

Isla nodded her head slowly in response to the man's question as she tried to figure out who he could possibly be. He was wearing what appeared to be a basketball top, white in colour with a blue stripe across the middle and a patch of red around the neck. Written across the front of the jersey was the word 'Wizards'. Below this, he was wearing blue jeans that appeared slightly too baggy for him and white trainers. He looks like a cross between a basketball player and a rapper, thought Isla. Over his left shoulder, was a grey and black rucksack, and in his right hand, was what appeared to be a wand. The man had a grey, bushy beard that came down just below his chin, and on his head, he was wearing a black baseball-style cap that also had the word 'Wizards' written across it in gold letters.

"Hey Isla, I hope I didn't startle you. I mean you no harm. My name is Steve, and I am friends with Wally."

The only Wally Isla knew was the wizard from Atalan. Surely, he couldn't mean him. Isla thought for a second; where had she heard the name Steve before? Then it came to her. Of course! Steve had been the wizard who had discovered the teleportation spell and had come to Earth. He was the person whose book Isla had found at her grandma's.

"Are you Steve the wizard? Are you from Atalan?" Isla asked.

"Yes, I am," beamed Steve, happy that Isla knew who he was and that he had come to the right place. "Can we talk? I really need your help," he continued.

Isla looked back towards the house. She knew her mum was in the office which was at the front of the house, and it was unlikely she would come out of there until her call was done, but Isla didn't want to take the risk. She ushered Steve towards the shed that was at the bottom corner of the garden.

"We can talk in there," Isla said.

The shed wasn't very big and had certainly seen better days. Inside, there were a few of her dad's tools, a lawn mower, Isla's bike and plenty of cobwebs and spiders. Before her trip to Atalan, Isla wouldn't have stepped foot in here as she didn't like creepy crawlies but after coming face to face with bullhounds, buzzagons, and goblins, a few little spiders didn't bother her in the slightest.

Once they were both inside, Isla closed the door behind them and turned to Steve.

"So, how did you get here, and how can I help you?" Isla asked. She had lots of questions for Steve but thought she would start with these two first.

"Well, a couple of days ago, I received an email from Wally telling me he thought he was in danger. He had heard a whisper that the goblins were planning on trying to take over Atalan and that they were marching towards Forest Glades and the Unkerdunkie village," said a concerned-looking Steve.

"But I thought the goblins had tried this before and had failed because they couldn't climb trees and had been driven back by the Unkerdunkies?" asked Isla, remembering the brief history of the Unkerdunkies that Oliver and Fartybubble had shared with her.

"Well, it seems this time they have some help. Did Wally ever mention anyone by the name of Warlock the sorcerer to you?"

Isla shook her head. She was pretty sure she would have remembered a name like that.

"Well, Warlock, as he likes to be known, is actually called Barry, and he was a wizard like Wally and me. Not long before I came to Earth, he was thrown out of the Magic Cone by the chief high wizard and banished to the outer parts of Atalan."

"What is the Magic Cone?" asked Isla, looking a little confused.

"The Magic Cone is an organisation that all wizards have to be a member of, and we have to follow the laws of the Cone; otherwise, we risk losing our wand and all our spell books and potions. One of the main rules of the Magic Cone is that wizards must not use their magic for evil or sell or supply potions or spells that could be used for evil doing.

"Barry was found to be selling his services to anyone who could afford it: bandits, goblins, he didn't care who used it as long as they could pay him. It sounds like he is up to his old tricks again. Somehow, he must have got hold of a wand, and he is helping the goblins with their invasion," Steve was looking more and more worried.

"So, how can I help you?" asked Isla.

"I haven't been able to get hold of Wally since his last message, and I fear the worst. I want to go back to Atalan to try and help him, plus I'm homesick. The only way I can get back is via the book you have."

"But how did you find me?" asked Isla.

She was struggling to take everything in that Steve was telling her. Standing in the shed talking to a wizard from Atalan was the last thing she had imagined she would be doing when she woke up this morning.

Steve brushed a couple of cobwebs out of his beard before he continued with his tale.

"As soon as you opened the book, it set off a tracking device which I've been able to monitor. All I had to do was put the address into Google Earth, print off a picture, and then sprinkle a drop of homemade teleportation potion onto it and hey presto!" Steve said with a smile.

"Where did you get the ingredients needed for the potion? I've never seen a buzzagon in this country before," said Isla, remembering back to everything she had to find to make the spell work back on Atalan.

Steve let out a little chuckle before answering.

"No, you're right, Isla, there are no buzzagons on Earth and not even Amazon sells goblin brew. I've been working for ages to come up with potions I can make using ingredients I can source over here. After a lot of trial and error, I finally succeeded in making a teleportation one. It's amazing what mixing together strawberries, sunflower seeds, a leaf from a silver birch, pidgin feathers, and a drop of homemade beer can achieve." As he spoke, he pulled out a fizzy drinks bottle from his rucksack that was filled to the top with a dark purple liquid.

Isla stood in silence for a second thinking about what she was going to do. Steve was obviously genuine. No one could just appear in her garden and know so much about Atalan if they weren't actually from there. If Wally and the Unkerdunkies were in danger, then, of course, she wanted to help in any way she could.

"Ok, I will fetch you the book. Wait here while I go and get it from my bedroom. I don't want my mum spotting you."

"That's great, Isla, thank you so much. Also, have you got anything else that might help me defeat Barry and his goblin horde?"

"Anything else? What sort of stuff do you need?" asked Isla.

"Well, weapons ideally," said Steve optimistically.

"Weapons!!" cried Isla. "I'm an 11-year-old girl, not Batman! Anyway, I thought you were a powerful wizard, and don't you have your wand for that?" she said, pointing to the brown wooden wand Steve was holding in his right hand.

"What, this thing?" he answered as he held up the wand and gave it a shake. "It's practically useless. I mean, it will work with potions, but I can't cast spells with it. I couldn't shoot lightning bolts or fireballs out of it, for example," said Steve, sounding disappointed.

11

"Why not?" asked Isla.

"Because it's made in China. I bought this from a gift shop in York. My real wand was snapped in half by my ex-wife during one of our heated discussions."

"Ex-wife?" asked Isla.

"Yes, unfortunately so," said Steve, looking a little upset. "When I first came to Earth, I met a beautiful girl within my first few days of arriving here. I fell in love, and that was the main reason I didn't return to Atalan. We got married after only a few months, and I set up my own business as a children's entertainer, doing a magic act at kids' parties and appearing at school fairs.

"Unfortunately, it didn't last. After a little while, we realised we both wanted different things. I wanted to be with her, and she wanted to be with a personal trainer from the local leisure centre. We had some blazing rows, and during one of them, she broke my wand.

"After that, my act suffered. I couldn't do the kind of tricks I used to. I had to resort to making balloon animals or pulling hankies out of my sleeve. Kids nowadays don't want that. They are only interested if you can walk through walls or on water or make the Statue of Liberty disappear. Then, there was the incident which resulted in a court case," as Steve spoke he looked down at the ground.

"Court case? What happened?" asked Isla a little nervously.

"Well, I was doing this kid's party in Manchester, and the birthday boy was getting very annoying, saying he knew how I was doing all my tricks. So I teleported him."

"Where to?"

"Bristol," said Steve with a slight smile on his face. "So, anyway, I have this outstanding case against me, so that's another good reason for me to return to Atalan."

"Right," said Isla nodding slowly. "I think I better go and get you that book."

Isla left Steve in the safety of the shed and disappeared inside the house. As she raced upstairs to her bedroom, she could hear her mum's voice coming from the office. She was deep in conversation and sounded like she would be on her call for some time. Isla dashed into her bedroom and grabbed the book from the shelf and took the key from her jewellery box before heading back downstairs. Within a matter of minutes, she was back inside the shed and handing the book to a very grateful-looking Steve.

"While you've been gone, I've been thinking," Steve said as he took the book from Isla and placed the fancy key into the lock of the book. "You should come with me," he said.

"What?" replied a very surprised Isla. "But why?" she asked.

"Well, if the goblins have got Wally and are trying to take over Atalan with the aid of Barry, then I could do with some help. You know your way around Atalan and know Wally and the Unkerdunkies," answered Steve.

"I'm not sure how much help I would be. I'm only eleven," replied Isla.

"Don't be modest now; I've heard the stories about your last trip to Atalan. How you and a couple of young Unkerdunkies were able to get all the ingredients needed for a teleportation spell. I know all too well how hard some of that stuff is to come by, and I'm a wizard with magic powers. I've been told all about how you overcame vinecatchers, outran buzzagons, befriended a giant troll and got in and out of the goblin kingdom without getting caught. You're a legend back in Atalan!" said Steve with a smile.

Isla blushed at the mention of her being a legend.

"I can't go again and risk getting stranded. I would love to help, but I'm scared about not being able to get back home to my family," said Isla looking sad.

"You won't get stranded. Remember," said Steve, holding up the fizzy drinks bottle and giving it a shake, "I've got enough potion in here for about 50 teleportation's. As long as you have a picture of home, you will be fine."

Isla thought long and hard about it. A chance to go back to Atalan and help her friends was very appealing. After all, they had helped her so much last time to get back home that she kind of felt she owed it to them. She was also pretty sure she would be back before anyone missed her. Last time she was in Atalan for a couple days, and when she returned, she had only been gone for a few minutes.

Her mum had said she would be in the office for a few hours, so using some quick maths that Isla did in her head, she had at least a week in Atalan. Steve already had the potion needed for her to get home, and she had pictures on her phone that she could use to get back. Although she did remember from last time how her phone had died just as the spell was being cast, and she had thought for one terrible moment she wouldn't be returning home.

"Ok, I will come," Isla said with a nod. She could already feel the excitement racing through her body. "I'm just going to run inside and grab a photo of home as well as get changed into some more sensible clothes," she said, looking down at her shorts, thin t-shirt and flip flops she was currently wearing.

"Great," said a very happy Steve. "You do that while I look through the book and find us somewhere safe to teleport to. We don't want to arrive in the Unkerdunkie village if the goblins are already there!"

And with that, Isla raced back inside to get ready for her return to Atalan.

Chapter 2

Isla stepped out of the white light and onto lush green grass; her arrival into Atalan was much smoother than last time: no falling through the air and landing on a poor unsuspecting Unkerdunkie on this occasion. The view that greeted her was absolutely breath-taking; she was stood looking out over a pool of water that was almost emerald in colour. Over to her right was a waterfall, the fast-flowing water crashing down over rocks and through the trees as it made its way to its final resting place in the lagoon below. Steve had picked this place from the pictures in the book to teleport to, as he said it was close enough to Wally's house but far enough away that if the goblins were there, then they wouldn't see them arrive.

"Ah, the Wizards Waterfall. I forgot how beautiful this place was," said Steve, admiring the view.

"Why is it called that?" asked Isla.

"Because the water here has healing powers, we use it a lot in our potions," as Steve spoke, he took his rucksack off his back and placed it on the floor before opening the main compartment. He took out another fizzy drinks bottle from the bag, only this one was empty.

Isla watched as he walked over to the edge of the lagoon and bent down and submerged the bottle into the emerald green water.

"I will take some with us; you never know when we might need some healing water," said Steve as he took the bottle out of the water, replaced the cap, and popped it back into his rucksack.

As he was doing this, Isla had taken a glance inside the open rucksack. It had looked like Steve had raided a joke shop. Inside were such items as stink bombs, bangers, and smoke bombs.

"What are they for?" asked Isla, pointing towards the contents of the rucksack.

"Oh those, they are just what I grabbed back on Earth that I thought might come in handy on this mission. I was a bit limited on what I could get hold of," said Steve with a shrug.

"Oh, I see," said Isla. "So, what's the plan?" she asked.

Steve zipped up his rucksack and placed it back on his back before answering.

"We will head to Wally's first; it's not far beyond those trees over there," he said as he pointed behind Isla and into the forest. "Depending what we find there, we'll decide what we do after," said the wizard.

Steve gave his rucksack a little shake to make sure it was secure and nothing could fall out before setting off towards the treeline and into the forest with Isla following closely behind.

They moved through the forest in silence, keeping an eye out for anything suspicious or any signs of goblins. After a short walk, they came across a clearing which Isla recognised immediately, although one thing had changed since the last time she had been here. The magic tree which had stood on its own in the middle of the clearing had been chopped down and had been stripped bare of its leaves.

Steve held up his hand and signalled Isla to stop.

"It looks like someone has beaten us here," he said as he dropped down onto one knee and surveyed the surroundings.

"What's happened to the magic tree?" asked Isla as she crouched down behind Steve.

"My guess is that Barry and the goblins have been here and that they have taken all the leaves and chopped the tree down to stop anyone from using it to create magic potions that could be used against them," said Steve stroking his beard as he spoke. "We need to be careful. They could still be here."

Isla felt her heart racing at the thought of coming face to face with the goblins again. She checked to make sure her phone and picture of home were still secured safely inside her jeans pocket. In case they had to make a quick getaway, she didn't want to risk them falling out.

"Right, Isla, follow me. We will go around the edge of the clearing and stay close to the trees just in case anyone is watching from Wally's house," whispered Steve as he beckoned Isla to follow him.

The pair moved slowly and as silently as possible, taking great care to avoid stepping on any twigs or getting caught up on any branches. After what felt like forever to Isla, they managed to circumnavigate the clearing without any drama and got within a few metres of Wally's front door. Once again, Steve raised his hand and dropped onto one knee with Isla doing the same close behind. From here, they could see that Wally's front door was slightly ajar and the splintered door frame suggested that it had been forced open.

"Right, Isla, I want you to wait here. Do not come inside until I tell you to, ok?" said Steve, looking slightly nervous.

Isla nodded. While she was happy to wait outside if there was potentially a horde of goblins on the other side of the door, she also felt scared for Steve.

The wizard pulled his rucksack off his back and took out a smoke bomb and a pack of bangers as well as the drinks bottle containing the teleportation potion which he passed to Isla. Along with this, he pulled his wand from out of the waistband of his jeans and handed that to her as well.

"If I'm not out after a few minutes or anything happens, then use these to get you home. Simply dip the wand into the potion and sprinkle the liquid onto your picture. Don't forget to say the magic words, 'Teleportation spell we are asking you, please take us off to somewhere new'."

"But..." before Isla had chance to argue that she didn't want to just leave him behind if he was in danger, Steve cut her off.

"No buts, you just focus on getting yourself home. I will be fine," said Steve, trying his best to reassure Isla.

And with that, he crept forwards towards the front door with his joke shop weapons in each hand moving stealthily like a basketball-playing ninja rapper. Once he reached the door, he crouched down and leant his left shoulder gently against it to ease it open slightly more. As he did so, the old wooden door let out a loud creak, and Isla held her breath, expecting any minute for a load of angry goblins to come charging out.

As soon as the door had opened slightly wider, Steve tossed in the smoke bomb and bangers before grabbing the door handle and pulling it shut. He held the handle tightly as the sound of bangers going off echoed from inside followed seconds later by smoke billowing out from under the door. As soon as this happened, Steve was in. He pushed the door open and burst inside, slamming it behind him as he went. Isla remained outside in her crouched position, using a bush for cover. After a few seconds, she was relieved to see the front door reopen, and Steve stood in the doorway beckoning her in.

"It's safe to enter, Isla. There is no one here; just be careful as it's a mess and there is lots of broken glass on the floor," warned Steve as he disappeared back inside the house.

As Isla entered the wizard's house, she was greeted by a scene of disarray: the house had been completely trashed. All over the floor was broken glass and books strewn everywhere, many of which had pages torn out and scattered all over the place. Most of the bookcases were now empty, and many of them had been knocked over and were now lying on the floor. The long table in the middle of the room glistened with the broken glass that now covered it; the contents of many jars and beakers had been spilled across the table top and were dripping onto the floor. The cauldron that once stood on the right of the room had also been pushed over leaving a large puddle of some mysterious liquid all over the stone floor.

Isla watched as Steve walked over to the shelves at the back of the room that last time she was here had been full of potions. Now they were completely bare. Steve then walked over to Wally's desk that had also been knocked over, scattering papers all around the room. In fact, one of the few things that was left standing was the wizard's three legged chair.

"Looks like they have taken all the potions as well as his laptop and destroyed all his spell books," said Steve surveying the room.

"What shall we do now?" asked Isla.

"Let's have a quick look around for anything that might be useful or give us a clue to Wally's whereabouts. Check the books, see if there are any guidebooks on Atalan, anything we can use to teleport," said Steve as he started rummaging through the papers littering the floor.

Isla started searching through the books that were now covering the floor, trying to find any that still had pages intact. She eventually found a few that hadn't been completely destroyed: one was about the flora and fauna of Atalan, one was a Haynes manual entitled 'Haynes explains how your wand works', and there was also a book on Sudoku. She also found a traveller's guide to Atalan which she handed over to Steve. He flicked through the pages of the book and gave an approving nod.

"This will do nicely; it has a picture of the chief high wizard's temple which could come in handy. Apart from this, it looks as though anything else of use has been taken. It's just a question of whether Wally has been taken as well, or did he escape before whoever it was arrived?" said Steve as he stroked his beard.

"So, now what?" asked Isla.

"Let's head towards the Unkerdunkies' village and see if the goblins have succeeded in invading it," said Steve as he stuffed the guidebook into his rucksack and then headed back towards the front door.

As Isla followed, she tripped on a loose piece of stone and stumbled forward. As she looked down to see what had caused her to stumble, she noticed the stone had been disturbed, and there was something hidden underneath it. She called to Steve to tell him to wait as she bent down to see what it was she had unearthed. From under the floor, she pulled out a bottle that contained a clear liquid which had a label stuck to the front with the letters SER written on it. She held it up for Steve to see.

"SER, whatever could that be?" said Steve as he took the bottle from Isla. He undid the top and took a sniff.

"Any idea what it is?" asked Isla.

"None at all, it doesn't smell of anything. It must be important, though; otherwise, Wally wouldn't have hidden it under the floor. I will take it with us, and hopefully, we can work out what it is," said Steve carefully placing the bottle into his ever expanding rucksack.

Once Steve was satisfied that there wasn't anything else hidden under the floor, the pair set off towards the Unkerdunkie village. Isla remembered her last journey this way and kept her eyes peeled, not only for any goblins or renegade wizards but also for those pesky vinecatchers!

Chapter 3

The last time Isla had walked through this part of
Forest Glades, it had been by lantern light and the
torch from her phone. It looked far less scary in the
daylight; in fact, this part of Atalan, like much of
what Isla had seen already, was beautiful. Trees of
all shapes and sizes that were densely-covered with
leaves of different shades of green stretched as far
as the eye could see. Long thin trees disappeared
high up into the sky; massive trees that had huge,
thick trunks that looked like they had been there for
many, many years; and much smaller trees that
would have looked great with a few baubles and
Christmas lights hanging off them.

As well as the vibrant greens, the forest was
awash with many other colours with an array of
beautiful flowers which grew on the bushes that
sprang up from in between the trees. Bright purple,
red, and yellow flowers were dotted all around, and
they glistened in the sunlight which penetrated
through the forest canopy.

The flowers not only looked great but they
also smelt divine, and as Isla walked through the
forest, her senses were truly indulged. She got a
whiff of mint, lavender and even sherbet as she
walked past one of the bushes that were covered in
purple flowers. It smelt so good it made Isla's

mouth water, and she wondered if this plant was actually edible.

"Hey Steve, what are those purple flowers that smell just like sherbet?" asked Isla.

"What is sherbet?" said Steve.

"It's a sweet; didn't you ever have it when you were on Earth?"

The wizard shook his head and screwed up his nose.

"I'm not a big fan of sweet stuff to be honest; I'm a more savoury person. Those purple flowers are called dinkydonks,"

"And can you eat them because they smell delicious," asked Isla.

"No, you can't eat dinkydonks. They would make you terribly ill and give you a really bad case of the squirty dance!"

"Oh," said Isla a little disappointed. She had no idea what the squirty dance was but it didn't sound very pleasant.

The sweet smell had made her realise though that she hadn't eaten lunch yet, and she was starting to get peckish. She tried to put the thought of food out of her mind as she continued along the track they were following.

The forest not only offered interesting sights and smells but also sounds. Isla could hear the chirping and whistling of what she could only imagine to be birds or something similar from high up within the trees. There was also plenty of

25

rustling coming from within the undergrowth from mysterious creatures who were hidden from view.

Since Steve didn't seem bothered by any of the sounds, Isla guessed that whatever was making them was probably harmless, but she stayed close to him as they moved along the track that cut through the middle of the forest just to be on the safe side.

Isla was careful to keep away from the edge of the track and the undergrowth that lined it as she remembered what happened last time she walked through here with Oliver and Fartybubble.

As she walked, a couple of bird-like creatures swooped down from the trees and flew across Isla and Steve's path before landing on a large branch opposite them. Their sudden appearance made Isla jump.

"Don't be scared, they are just gurwaver birds," said Steve.

The birds were of a similar size to a crow, although they were far more colourful. Their bodies were a bright red and their wings a mixture of red, green, and blue feathers. On their head, a strip of blue feathers stood proud, making the gurwaver bird appear to have a Mohawk.

"Beautiful creature, the gurwaver bird," said Steve, "and fun fact for you, they can actually fly for days on end without having to land or to stop for food or water. And you can make some amazing spells with their spit. Fascinating creatures, absolutely fascinating."

After a spot of bird-watching, the pair continued along the track and towards the Unkerdunkie village. They hadn't gone much further when there was a loud rustling from the undergrowth and a group of furry animals who looked a little like a mop on legs appeared and darted across in front of Isla and Steve before disappearing back into the undergrowth on the other side of the track. This time, Isla recognised the creatures.

"Were they furbles?" asked Isla. She remembered her last visit to Atalan and meeting Fartybubble' s pet furble, Mopsy.

"Yes, they were. They make lovely pets but wild ones are very shy," replied Steve.

They continued down the track for a while longer before they reached the edge of the Unkerdunkie village. Isla was glad that there had been no run-ins with any vinecatchers and that the journey had passed without incident.

As they approached the village, Steve signalled a halt and crouched down behind a large tree that jutted out onto the track.

"The Unkerdunkies' village is just up ahead. We need to move very carefully now just in case the goblins are already here," whispered Steve.

"And what's the plan if they are here?" asked Isla, feeling a little nervous.

"I've no idea," said Steve, shrugging his shoulders.

And with that, he set off towards the village, staying as low as he could and moving slowly. Isla did the same, keeping her head down as much as possible to the point where she was almost crawling. Through the trees up ahead came the sound of laughing and shouting, although Isla couldn't make out what was being said as it wasn't in a language she recognised. Suddenly, Steve spun around and grabbed Isla's arm and pulled her off the track and into the undergrowth. Isla's first thought was that she hoped there weren't any vinecatchers lurking in here. Her second thought was why was she now lying in a bush?!

"The goblins are already here, look!" said Steve, as he parted the bush so Isla could see through it.

Isla peered through the gap and was shocked at what she saw. The Unkerdunkie village was teaming with goblins. They were everywhere, lying against tree trunks drinking their goblin brew, dancing and shouting on the forest floor and riding the lifts that took them up into the village above. What was even more surprising than the sight of the goblins though, was that the Unkerdunkies were there as well, and they appeared to be waiting on the goblins hand and foot.

Isla could see Unkerdunkies appearing with buckets of water, obviously fetched from a nearby stream, and being emptied into a giant trough for the goblins to drink out of. Others appeared carrying baskets overflowing with red berries while a couple of Unkerdunkies even used large leaves to fan some of the goblins who were lying in the sunshine.

"What is going on?" asked a very confused Isla.

"It looks like the Unkerdunkies have been put under some sort of spell so that they will do exactly what they are told. Looks like Barry's handiwork to me," said Steve as he surveyed the scene in front of him.

"Can you undo the spell?" asked Isla hopefully.

Steve shook his head before answering.

"No, not with a pretend wand and the contents of a joke shop. We would need to know what spell was used and then try and work out some kind of antidote. I think it's time we paid the high wizard a visit and asked for some help," said Steve as he opened his bag and rummaged through it, looking for the travel guide.

As Steve searched through the rucksack, Isla continued to scan the Unkerdunkie village trying to spot any familiar faces. Just as she was about to give up, something caught her eye. One of the Unkerdunkies carrying a bucket of water had stopped for a second to rest. He had placed his bucket on the floor and had taken his hat off to mop his brow and wipe sweat out of his blonde hair.

"Oliver," whispered Isla. It took all her restraint not to shout over to him.

He was wearing the traditional Unkerdunkie clothing, as he had been the last time Isla had seen him. He hadn't appeared to have grown much if at all and still looked to be a fair bit shorter than her. Facially, though, he looked slightly older, and the first signs of a beard seemed to be forming with a few blonde wisps of hair on his chin. Isla continued to scan the forest floor looking for his brother, but there was no sign of Fartybubble. She looked up into the trees to see if she could spot him high up in the village itself. There was no sign of him, but she did see something else.

"Wally," said Isla in a hushed tone. She tapped Steve on his shoulder and pointed to where his wizard friend was.

Wally was sat cross-legged in a cage that appeared to be made from branches and which was suspended high above the forest floor between two large trees. He was wearing his purple gown, although he appeared to be missing his hat as well as his wand.

"Well, that answers the question of where's Wally," said Steve with a sigh.

"Why is he locked up in a cage unlike the Unkerdunkies?" asked Isla.

"Because Barry's spell won't work on him. Wizards have different rankings depending on their experience, skill level, and powers. Wally, like me, is ranked as a pro. When Barry was banished, he had his ranking reduced to a noob. A lower-ranking wizard is unable to cast a spell on a higher-ranking one; hence why Wally has been locked in a cage. They've obviously captured him and taken away his wand and all his potions so that he can't fight them. Without Wally to help us, we definitely need the help of the chief high wizard," said Steve.

As he spoke, he pulled out the travel guide from his rucksack along with the bottle that contained the teleportation spell. He flicked through the pages of the book until he came to one that had a picture of what appeared to Isla to be a magnificent temple. It reminded her of the Taj Mahal which she had been learning about recently at school.

Steve poured a little of the potion onto his wand and held it over the page of the travel guide.

"Are you ready?" he asked Isla.

Isla took one last look over to the Unkerdunkie village. She felt sad that she was about to leave her friends behind under the spell of the goblins and an evil wizard, but she knew that there was nothing she could do for now to help. She just hoped that whoever this chief high wizard was that they could put a stop to this.

Isla nodded to Steve that she was ready to go, but as she did, there was a commotion from within the village. It appeared that a couple of the Unkerdunkies had spotted Isla and Steve's hiding place and were now frantically pointing towards the bushes and shouting for the goblins to come and investigate.

Two goblins got up from their spot from under a large tree where they had been taking a nap. They grabbed their weapons and came charging over.

Isla looked at Steve who was still holding his wand over the picture of the temple.

"What are you waiting for? Cast the spell," whispered Isla.

The goblins had now reached the edge of the bushes and had begun hacking away at them with their very sharp weapons.

"I can't. I've forgotten the spell," replied Steve who was now looking very worried.

"What do you mean you've forgotten it? You cast it to get us here in the first place!"

"I know, but my mind goes blank when I get flustered," Steve looked very flushed and sweat was pouring down his face.

The bush that Steve and Isla had been hiding behind was now almost completely gone, chopped away by the angry pair of goblins who were screaming and shouting at them.

Isla grabbed the wand off Steve and held it over the guidebook and gave it a little shake. As a droplet of potion fell onto the page, Isla shouted out the spell.

"Teleportation spell we are asking you, please take us off to somewhere new."

The page immediately came to life. Isla grabbed Steve by the arm and pulled him towards the white light that was now shining brightly out of the book. They disappeared just as the two goblins came crashing through the bush, swinging their weapons with all their might.

Chapter 4

As Isla stepped out of the white light, she was confronted by an amazing sight. A huge temple that looked like it was made entirely out of gold stood in front of her glistening in the sunlight. A cobbled path lined with immaculately trimmed bushes either side led you up to a small set of steps that appeared to take you into the temple through a large archway. As Isla was taking in her new surroundings, two figures appeared in front of her.

"Halt, who goes there!?" shouted the two strangers in unison.

Isla breathed a sigh of relief that the two figures were not the goblins from the village.

Instead, a man and a woman blocked Isla and Steve's path. Both were dressed almost identical with a black jacket and white shirt on with a thick red belt around their waists. The man wore black trousers that had sequins along the side that ran all the way down to some of the shiniest black shoes that Isla had ever seen. The woman was wearing black shorts and tights along with black boots that came up to just below her knees. Both of them were also wearing black top hats that had a red feather sticking out from the top. In their hands, they held a long wooden staff each, which had a large crystal at the end that intermittently flashed red. These staffs were currently being pointed quite menacingly in Isla and Steve's direction.

"My name is Wizard Steve, and I am a member of the Magic Cone. I wish to speak to the chief high wizard regarding Warlock the sorcerer and his plans to take over Atalan," Steve held up his hands as he spoke to show that he came in peace.

The two staff-wielding strangers looked Steve up and down and then looked at each other before the man turned back to Steve and spoke.

"You don't look much like a wizard to me. If you are a member of the Magic Cone, then tell me the secret password."

Isla looked over at Steve. The man was right, he really didn't look like a wizard in his current attire. She just hoped that he knew the secret password.

"Abracadabra," said Steve proudly.

Isla looked back over at the two black-clad individuals, they both nodded and smiled. Surely that wasn't the secret password to the Magic Cone. It is hardly very original, Isla thought to herself.

"Follow us, we will take you through to the chief," said the woman.

And with that, the pair lowered their staffs, turned around and walked off down the cobbled path signalling for Steve and Isla to follow.

"Who are they?" whispered Isla as she walked alongside Steve towards the golden temple.

Steve didn't answer. He was too busy staring at the woman who was leading the way, like a love-struck teenager.

"Steve," Isla whispered again.

"She's beautiful," said Steve before realising he had said that out loud. He blushed slightly before continuing.

"Oh yes, they are the chief high wizard's assistants; all the best wizards and magicians have assistants. They are like her personal bodyguards. They are trained in both magic and martial arts and are experts in the wizards' fighting system of staffjitsu. They could easily turn you into a frog and kick your butt at the same time!" said Steve with a chuckle.

As they neared the temple, Isla could see just what an amazing building it really was. Above the archway that led you inside was a giant dome that sparkled in the sunlight as if it had been sprinkled with diamonds. Either side of the dome were two smaller ones that also glistened in the light. At the front of the temple were eight giant windows: four across the top and four along the bottom, each one with tinted glass so that you couldn't see inside.

Isla and Steve were led up the steps and under the archway and through an already opened pair of large red double doors, each one with a huge gold handle. The inside of the temple was just as jaw-dropping as the outside. The hallway Isla found herself in was massive. She was pretty sure she could fit her entire house in this one room. In the middle of the hall was a red-carpeted staircase that led you straight up to the floor above. Hanging from the ceiling was a couple of giant ornate chandeliers that were covered in crystals and lights that were made to look like candles. The walls were covered in paintings depicting animals, landscapes, and wizards, and dotted around the hall were many beautifully carved stone statues.

Isla spotted another couple of assistants stood just inside the hallway that were dressed the same as the pair they had followed. Both were holding their staffs across their chests and were stood to attention.

"This way, please," said the female assistant as she pointed off to a corridor that was beyond the staircase to the right.

"Of course," said Steve with a huge smile on his face. "And what is your name?" he asked.

"I am Matilda, and this is Noel," answered the assistant, pointing to her partner.

"Lovely to meet you, Matilda,"

Isla rolled her eyes at Steve's obvious attempt to chat her up.

The corridor, like the stairs, was covered in a red carpet, and as Isla walked across it, she felt as if her trainers were disappearing into it as it was that soft underfoot. The walls of the corridor were covered in paintings as well as large glass cabinets that were filled with beautifully-crafted wands and staffs.

The corridor took many twists and turns along the way, and they passed numerous doors leading off it. Each one was shut tight and looked the same as the last. They were all wooden with a gold doorknob, and each one had a gold nameplate in the centre of the door which told you which room it led too. Isla noticed that they passed a wand room, staff room, the potion making room, a gym, library and even a home cinema room.

It felt like they had been walking for miles when, eventually, they came to a wooden door at the end of the corridor which read, 'Throne room'.

"Wait here, please," said Noel before knocking on the door.

"Enter," came a female's voice from the other side.

Noel opened the door and disappeared inside, closing it behind him and leaving Matilda with Steve and Isla, much to Steve's joy. After a few moments, the door reopened, and Noel ushered the pair into the throne room.

"The chief high wizard will see you now."

As Isla stepped inside the room, she was hit by the whiteness of it all: white tiles on the floor with bright white walls and ceiling. It took a moment for her eyes to adjust to the brightness of it, and she wished she had her sunglasses with her.

The room was large and square-shaped, and apart from a few objects that were dotted around, it was fairly bare. On the wall to the right hung a large ornate mirror, and to the left-hand side of the room stood what appeared to be a pool table. Isla wasn't an expert on pool. She had played a few games against her parents on some of their holidays, but she did know that pool tables had four legs. This one, like Wally's chair, had only three legs and yet, like the wizard's chair, it hadn't toppled over.

The green cloth that covered the table was covered in balls, although unlike the game that Isla had played back home, all the balls on this table were blue. Hanging on the wall behind the three-legged pool table was a cabinet that was full of cues and chalk.

Stood next to this cabinet was a machine that looked very much like the arcade games that Isla would play in the amusements every time she visited the seaside with her parents. Unlike those machines though, instead of pictures of spaceships and aliens plastered all over it, this one was covered in drawings depicting wizards battling goblins, which seemed very apt, thought Isla.

Running down the middle of the room was a strip of red carpet which made Isla think of the red stripe which ran through the bright white toothpaste she used at home. Stood either side of the carpet were more assistants dressed in the same black uniform, although Isla did notice that they all had different coloured feathers in their hats. Isla counted ten in total, five on each side, forming a guard of honour. The red strip of carpet ran all the way to the back of the room where it came to a stop at a couple of low steps that led up to a small platform. On top of this was a large gold throne and in it sat who Isla presumed to be the chief high wizard herself.

She was the most beautiful woman Isla had ever seen, with supermodel looks and the kind of beauty that could get her, her own reality television show, thought Isla. She was dressed all in white to go with the rest of the room and looked like a beautiful bride to be. Her long white dress flowed all the way down to the floor and appeared to be made from pure silk. On her head, she wore the traditional-looking wizard's hat that was covered in tiny gems and jewels that sparkled with different colours every time she moved. Under her hat flowed long brown locks of thick hair that fell down past her shoulders and shimmered in the light, at times looking like it had almost a tint of green in it. Around her neck, she wore a silver necklace with a large red stone attached to it, and in her right hand, she held a golden wand.

Steve approached the throne, and Isla followed closely behind. As they got within a few steps of the platform, the chief high wizard held up her hand to signal them to stop.

"Wizard Steve, to what do I owe this pleasure? I thought you had settled on Earth. And who is your companion that you bring to my temple?" The chief asked, glancing over towards Isla.

Isla watched Steve do a weird sort of bow and curtsy combination before he answered.

"Your Highness, I have returned to Atalan after receiving an urgent email from Wizard Wally regarding a plot by Warlock the sorcerer to take over our beautiful kingdom. This is Isla who has accompanied me from Earth to help me on my quest."

"So, you are the Earth child I have heard so much about, who has already visited Atalan before and made quite a name for herself," said the chief, staring intently at Isla.

Isla didn't really know what she was meant to do when addressing a chief high wizard: should she curtsy or bow or do the strange thing Steve had done? Should she address her as your highness or ma'am or something completely different? Instead, she just found herself blushing and nodding in response to the chief's question.

"Well, let me take this opportunity to personally welcome you back to our wonderful kingdom, and I hope you enjoy your stay. Now Steve, please tell me about this plot concerning Warlock the sorcerer. What has old Bazza been up to now?" she asked as she sat back on her throne.

Steve proceeded to tell her everything he knew so far: the email from Wally that had told him about Barry's plot to invade Atalan with the help of the goblins; how they had visited Wally's house and had found him missing and the place ransacked; then the visit to the Unkerdunkie village where they had seen the goblins, and the Unkerdunkies seemingly under their spell; and finally, seeing Wally being held prisoner and locked up in a cage.

The chief tapped her chin with her wand and looked lost in thought for a few moments before she finally answered.

"Well now, this is a little concerning. I wonder where Barry has been able to get hold of a wand to enable him to cast such spells. No matter, we will soon put a stop to this nonsense. First, I need to find out where he is," as she spoke, the chief pulled out a white object from underneath her throne.

The object looked to Isla to be a tablet, the type her mum and dad used for work and that she was allowed to use occasional for playing games on. Isla watched the chief swipe her finger numerous times across the screen as if she was looking for something.

"Now that's odd," the chief said, looking a little confused.

"Is everything ok, Your Wizardness?" asked Matilda.

"Well, if Barry is using a wand, then he has been able to disarm the tracker as I cannot find it on the 'track-my-wand' app," said the chief as she stared long and hard at the tablet's screen.

"Tracker?" said Steve, looking slightly confused.

"Yes, Steve, a tracker. All wands have an inbuilt tracker in them so I can monitor where they are and how they are being used at all times. Only I and my assistants know about these trackers and how to disable them so it seems strange that I cannot locate Barry's. Never mind though, all is not lost, I will find him the old fashioned way," and with that, the chief got up out of her throne.

Isla watched on in amazement as the chief appeared to literally float down the steps and across the floor over towards the large mirror that was hanging on the wall. The bottom of her dress just skimmed the ground as she glided gracefully across the room.

The mirror was bigger than the chief herself and had an ornate gold frame surrounding it. The chief pointed her wand at the centre of the mirror and spoke:

"Mirror, mirror, let me look

Where is Barry

That naughty wizard?"

Isla watched, thinking that maybe the chief needed to work on her rhyming, as the mirror burst into life. Where once there was a reflection of the chief suddenly became a swirl of light followed by a completely different image. The mirror now showed a horde of goblins led by a very familiar person.

"Fizzbit," whispered Isla at the sight of the giant troll leading the goblin army.

Sat on Fizzbit's shoulders was a character Isla didn't recognise; he looked a bit like a younger Wally. He was dressed all in red: a red gown, boots and wizard's hat. The only other colour on his outfit were the yellow flashes across his gown and hat that resembled lightning bolts. His long brown beard was in two plaits that came almost down to his stomach. In his right hand he held a wand which he was using to urge Fizzbit onwards, much like a jockey uses a riding crop on a horse.

"It seems that our friend Barry has quite the army to help him. And it looks to me that he is heading towards the elves' settlement," said the chief as she studied the image in front of her.

"Your Wizardness, please let me go and put a stop to this at once," said one of the chief's assistants, stepping forwards out of the guard of honour line that she had been stood in.

She was dressed the same as the other assistants although seemed to be the only one that had a black feather in her hat which she wore on top of a mound of bright red hair. She also had some of the most piecing green eyes that Isla had ever seen.

"Now that is a great idea, Ivana," said the chief, looking over to her assistant before turning to Steve.

"I mean, I would love to go myself, Steve, but I have a gym session with my personal trainer booked later on, and I really can't miss it. I have a holiday on the beach at Wonderlush Bay in a few weeks, and you know what they say, 'You can't miss the gym if you want to stay trim'," she said, flexing her biceps.

Steve just smiled and nodded in agreement. Looking at the chief, she never misses a gym session, thought Isla to herself, going by her defined arms that rippled with muscle in her sleeveless dress.

"Ivana is my top assistant. She is a black feather in staffjitsu. Barry's magic will be no match for her, and with her skill and powers, she can easily take on a horde of goblins. I suggest you go to the elves' settlement and wait for them there," said the chief to Ivana.

"Make sure all the elves stay indoors so they don't get caught up in the magical crossfire. Ivana, I want you to capture Barry and the goblins and bring them back here. Barry will be made to undo his spell and release the Unkerdunkies and Wally before being placed in the temple's prison. The goblins will be sent back to their kingdom where they will be placed under house arrest. That is where they will stay so that once again Atalan will be a safe place to live," said the chief, looking very pleased with herself.

Isla smiled to herself. The plan sounded so simple, and she was hopeful that it wouldn't be long before she could spend some time with her friends, the Unkerdunkies, Wally, and Fizzbit before returning safely home.

"I am ready to go and do your bidding, Your Wizardness," said Ivana as she did the strange curtsy bow combination that Steve had done earlier.

"Thank you, Ivana. Steve, why don't you and Isla accompany her? You can help keep the elves out of the way while Ivana takes care of Barry," said the chief.

"Yes, of course. Maybe Matilda should come as well. We might need an extra pair of hands?" said Steve hopefully.

"No need. Ivana is more than a match for Barry and his army," said the chief.

"Ok," nodded Steve a little disappointed. "I have a teleportation spell we can use to get to the elves' settlement," he added excitedly, holding up his rucksack.

"No need, my dear, you can simply step through the mirror," said the chief as she pointed her wand towards it.

Isla watched as the image of Barry and the goblins changed to a field of long grass with trees dotted around the edge.

"Right, I will leave you to it. I'm off to feel the burn," and with that, the chief floated across the room and out of the door.

"Are we ready to go?" asked Ivana.

Isla looked over to Steve who was once again staring over towards Matilda.

"Steve?" whispered Isla.

"Oh yes, yes, I am ready," stuttered Steve.

"Let's go then," said Ivana as she stepped towards the mirror and disappeared through it.

Chapter 5

Isla was starting to get used to this mode of transport now, whether it was stepping into a book, a phone, or now a mirror. She wished you could teleport back on Earth as it would certainly make going on holiday abroad a much simpler task.

After stepping through the mirror, Isla found herself stood in a field of very long grass. It was so long it came up to almost her shoulders. Around the edge of the field stood a number of large trees that appeared to be evenly spaced apart.

"Follow me," said Ivana as she set off towards one of the trees.

Ivana led the way followed by Steve with Isla bringing up the rear. As they got closer towards the tree, Isla noticed that there was a small door cut into the bottom of the trunk. As well as the door, there were a few small glass windows going all the way up the trunk. It appeared that people actually lived inside these trees.

"Is this where the elves live?" Isla whispered to Steve up ahead.

"Yes, this is their settlement. All these trees around here are their homes," said Steve pointing around the edge of the field.

As the trio got closer to the trees, the long grass fell away to a much more normal length. In fact, the grass around the base of the trees was short and well kept. The lines of different shades of green suggested it was lovingly cared for and mowed regularly. As Isla walked under one of the overhanging branches of the tree they were heading for, she felt her foot catch on something on the ground. She bent down to investigate what it was, only to discover a thin wire that seemed to be attached between the trunks of two of the trees. Ivana and Steve had somehow managed to step over the wire without touching it.

While Isla was bent down examining the wire, she heard a sound above her like something had fallen out of the tree followed by a whoosh as an object flew over her head. The next sound was an "oomph" accompanied by Steve lying in a heap on the floor. Swinging above him was a thick rope dangling from one of the branches above and attached to this rope was what looked like a giant Wellington boot! It seemed that what Isla had caught her foot on was some kind of trip wire that had set off a booby trap.

"Ha-ha, my trap worked, that was sick, man, sick!" came a voice from behind the tree.

As Isla helped Steve up from off the floor and replaced his cap back on his head, a small boy appeared from behind the tree trunk. He was dressed almost identical to that of an Unkerdunkie, with a green tunic and red belt, green and white hooped trousers and a red hat complete with green bobble. He was very small in stature and much shorter than both Oliver and Fartybubble although facially he looked a similar age. Under his hat you could make out tight black curly hair along with piecing blue eyes. Whoever this boy was, he seemed very happy with himself as a big smile filled his caramel-skinned face.

"I'm sorry about that, bro. I didn't mean any harm. It's just that we elves love a good prank. I'm Benji, by the way, who are you guys?" said the mischievous little elf looking at the trio stood in front of him.

"I am Ivana, and I am the chief high wizard's number one assistant."

"No way. That's amazing! Are you from the magic temple then?" shouted Benji as he hopped around in excitement.

Ivana just nodded in response, her face completely emotionless.

"So, that means you're a master of staffjitsu. I bet you could kick some serious butt!" as Benji spoke, he threw his arms and legs around as if he was fighting an imaginary opponent.

"Well, you might get to see soon enough," replied Ivana with a wry smile.

"And how about you, dude, have you just stepped off the court?" said Benji looking over to Steve. As he spoke, he mimed throwing a basketball.

"Court?" replied Steve, a little confused by the question.

"Yeah, have you been on the court playing some b-ball, shooting some hoops?" asked Benji as he carried on his imaginary game of basketball.

Steve was still none the wiser and looked over to Isla, hoping that she might know what he was talking about.

"I believe he's on about your top. He seems to think you've been playing basketball," said Isla, pointing to Steve's basketball jersey.

"Oh, right," said Steve with a nod, "ha-ha no, I've not been playing basketball. I'm actually a wizard. My name is Steve."

"And what about you, young lady, are you some kind of magic person as well?" Benji asked Isla.

"No, nothing like that," said Isla shaking her head, "my name is Isla, and I'm from Earth."

"Whoa now, are you the Earth girl I've heard about who broke into the goblin kingdom with a couple of Unkerdunkies?" asked a surprised-looking Benji.

Isla found herself blushing again. She was amazed by the amount of people who had heard about her previous exploits in Atalan.

"Yes, that's right," she replied, nodding.

"Well, hats off to you then. You must have some great leadership skills because those Unkerdunkies are not known for being very courageous. Not like us elves. They just like to dress similar and make people think they are like us."

Isla wasn't sure who dressed like who, but remembering back to her first encounter with Oliver, it certainly seemed like there was no love lost between the Unkerdunkies and the elves.

"So, what brings a chief high wizard's assistant, a wizard, and a girl from Earth to our little settlement? If we had known you were coming, I would have removed the booby traps and put up some bunting," said Benji with a smile,

"Well, at this moment in time, the great Warlock the sorcerer is heading towards your little settlement with an army of goblins intent on taking over your land," said Ivana, rather menacingly, Isla thought for someone who was meant to be here to protect the elves.

"Wait, what?! Goblins coming here, but why?! We haven't done anything to them. We are just mischievous and loveable elves who don't want any trouble," said Benji, looking very worried. All the talk of how courageous the elves were seemed to have been forgotten for the time being.

"Do not worry, Ivana is here to stop them and to keep you and your people safe," said Steve, trying to put the elf's mind at rest.

"Well, that's not entirely true," as Ivana spoke she turned around to face Steve and Isla, the now glowing end of her staff pointing menacingly towards them.

"What do you mean?" asked Steve.

"Well, who do you think provided Warlock with his wand and removed the tracker from it?" as Ivana spoke, a smile spread across her face. Isla was expecting this to be followed by a menacing laugh and for her to rub her hands together in glee at any moment, like some kind of super villain from the movies.

Steve's expression changed from a look of confusion to that of anger as the penny dropped, and he realised just what Ivana meant.

"You?! But why?" said Steve.

"Because I'm fed up with being nothing more than an assistant. All the chief high wizard does all day is sit on her throne and order us around. She goes to the gym for an hour each day, and the rest of the time she binges on box sets. I want to do that!" said a very animated Ivana.

"I knew we would have been better off bringing Matilda," fumed Steve.

"Umm, can someone tell me exactly what is going on here and whether I can leave as it's almost my bath time," said a very confused-looking Benji.

Isla was also a little confused, as well as starting to become slightly worried that her journey home may not be as straightforward as it had first appeared.

"Let me explain to you all exactly what is going on," said Ivana, motioning with her staff for the three of them to sit down. Once they were all seated and she had their attention, she continued.

"I am a black feather in staffjitsu, the most powerful of the assistants, and yet my work is nothing more than babysitting the chief high wizard, trying to remove stains from all her white outfits and occasionally helping her perform a spell. I have all this power, and it's time for me to use it.

"After Warlock the sorcerer was banished, he wanted his revenge, so I contacted him via WizardBook and offered to help. I couldn't take over Atalan from inside the temple where I'm constantly being watched, but someone on the outside could as long as they had the right tools. Once Warlock had the wand that I stole from the temple, and we had created a spell that would put everyone and everything in Atalan under our powers, then we were good to go. The goblins didn't need much convincing to help. They love a good invasion anyway. We already have the Unkerdunkies under our command; next it will be the elves and the fairies. Before long we will control all the races in Atalan, the Bandits, the Bushwhackers and even the Mistgiants. Everyone will succumb to our spell, and once we have our army, we will dethrone the chief high wizard and claim the temple as ours," this time Ivana did finish with a menacing laugh that sent shivers down Isla's spine.

"You will never get away with it!" shouted Steve.

"Oh really, and who is going to stop us? You and your child's wand?!" laughed Ivana, pointing at the toy wand that was sticking out of Steve's waistband.

"Maybe your friend Wally?" said Ivana sarcastically, "He was the first one we captured. We heard a rumour that he had somehow discovered our plans and was in the process of making a serum that would counteract our spell. We should have known that was nonsense. That washed-up wizard is still making spells to start tantrums and creating potions for curing hiccups. His powers are no match for us, and he is now safely trapped inside a cage, swinging from the trees like a pet daggermoth."

At the mention of the word serum, Steve and Isla both looked at each other. Of course, the bottle they had found hidden under the floor labelled SER was in fact a serum to fight this spell. Wally must have quickly hidden it before his house had got raided. The serum was still inside the rucksack that Steve was wearing on his back.

"What's that?" shouted Benji, leaping up from his seated position and pointing out across the field in the direction that Isla and her companions had just come from.

"Sit down," commanded Ivana with a wave of her staff. Benji's bottom hit the ground in a flash.

55

Isla and Steve were now looking out in the direction that Benji had pointed and could see exactly what had made the little elf react in such a way. Heading across the field towards them was a small army of goblins and leading the way was Fizzbit with Barry riding high on his shoulders.

Ivana turned to face the oncoming goblins and her new best friend, Barry, and smiled.

"Warlock has arrived," she said with a cackle.

She is getting more like an over-the-top super villain by the second, Isla thought to herself.

With Ivana distracted for a moment, Steve used the opportunity to slide the rucksack off his back and undo the main compartment. He slowly slid his hand inside and fished around trying to find the bottle of serum that was tucked away amongst the smoke bombs and bangers. As his hand fell upon what he thought was the bottle of serum, Ivana glanced back around and spotted him.

"And what do you think you're doing? I hope you are not thinking of making a grab for that teleportation spell you have stashed in there and trying to make a run for it, because I can assure you it's pointless. In fact, hand over that bag," said Ivana, holding out her left hand while using her right hand to point the staff directly at Steve.

Steve let out a sigh before handing over his rucksack to Ivana. As he lifted the bag with his left hand and passed it to her, he used his right hand to slip the bottle of serum and a few joke shop goodies out of it and hide them behind his back. It was the kind of sleight of hand trick that may have worked with a bunch of five-year-olds at a children's party, but it wasn't going to work with an assistant to a chief high wizard.

Ivana shook her head and looked at Steve with contempt.

"Do you really think you can fool me with the oldest trick in the book? Whatever you have behind your back, hand it over now before I turn all three of you into frogs!"

"Ok, you can have it," said Steve.

As the last word left his mouth, Steve quickly brought his right hand from behind his back and in one fluid movement, he launched a mixture of bangers, smoke and stink bombs directly at Ivana. There was a loud bang followed by a plume of smoke accompanied by a putrid smell of rotten eggs that filled the air.

"Isla, take this and run! Go and get help," shouted Steve, throwing the bottle of serum over to Isla.

As soon as the bottle had left Steve's hand, he was up on his feet. He dived forwards through the smoke and made a lunge for Ivana's staff. A struggle ensued although Isla didn't have a clue what was going on through the thick cloud of smoke that had covered the area. Isla wasn't sure if Steve had been shopping at his local joke shop or military base, but she wasn't going to hang about to ask. She was up on her feet in a flash, gripping the bottle of serum tightly in her left hand. She raced over to Benji who was still sat down looking shocked and confused. Isla grabbed him by his arm and scooped him up onto his feet.

"Come on, we need to get out of here," shouted Isla.

Before Benji had chance to reply, Isla was pulling him away from the commotion and sprinting off through the trees, dragging him behind. Isla hated the thought of leaving Steve, but she didn't really have any choice. She needed to get away from Ivana, Barry and the approaching goblin army and somehow find help. How she wished she had Oliver and Fartybubble with her in this moment in time.

Chapter 6

As Isla ran through the trees away from Ivana and the approaching goblins, she felt Benji struggling and trying to free himself from her grip on his arm. She spun around to see what the problem was.

"Come on, Benji, we need to go! What's wrong?" shouted Isla.

Benji was flailing his arms around to try and break Isla's grip and was attempting to run back the way they had come and straight towards Ivana. The little elf looked at Isla with tears in his eyes.

"I can't leave my family behind to be captured by the evil wizards and goblins and to be put under their spell. I need to save them," pleaded Benji.

"There is nothing we can do. If we stay, then we will be captured as well and put under the spell and then who will save Atalan?" said Isla.

Like Benji, Isla really didn't want to run away and leave Steve and the elves behind to be captured, but she had no other options. They needed to escape and try and find someone who could help them.

"If you want to help rescue your family, then we need to get away," said Isla, grabbing Benji by his shoulders and looking straight into his tear-filled eyes.

Benji looked back towards the elf settlement through the smoke that still clung in the air. They could now make out the pursuing goblins who were closing in. He turned back to face Isla and nodded.

"Ok, let's get out of here. But you need to follow me as there are booby traps all over the place."

Isla smiled and nodded as Benji grabbed her by the hand and led the way. He set off, sidestepping, ducking and jumping over invisible traps. Isla carefully followed his every step as she didn't want to end up in a heap on the floor after being wiped out by a Wellington boot, and especially not when the goblins were in hot pursuit.

As they moved, Isla heard a couple of yells and screams from behind them. She looked back over her shoulder to see who had made the sounds and was pleased to see that some of the goblins had encountered a couple of Benji's booby traps. There was a giant hole in the ground that had once been covered by leaves and twigs that was now home to four or five goblins. There was a large rope attached to a branch of a nearby tree that now had an upside-down goblin suspended from it by his foot. Another goblin was lying face first in the grass with a boot firmly wedged in its bottom. Isla had no idea where the boot had come from nor did she care!

The booby traps were working, not only in capturing and disabling the goblins, but also in slowing them down as the remaining ones moved at a snail's pace to avoid becoming the next victim of a mischievous little elf's prank.

"This way," shouted Benji as he pulled Isla down a small slope and came to a stop by a pile of twigs that were in a heap on the floor.

Benji got to work straight away removing the twigs and throwing them to the side.

"Quick, give me a hand," he said to Isla.

Isla joined in, and within no time, the pile of twigs had gone and all that was left was a giant hole in the ground.

"We can escape through here. The goblins will never be able to follow us," said Benji pointing into the hole.

"Through there?" said Isla, looking down at the large black hole by her feet.

Isla wasn't a big fan of the dark or of confined spaces, so the thought of disappearing down into some pitch black underground tunnel wasn't her idea of fun.

"Yeah, I always use these tunnels to go and visit my friends. I usually have a lantern with me so I can see, but I'm sure I will be able to find my way even in the dark," said Benji with a smile.

Isla didn't want to take the risk of getting lost, and if she was going down a tunnel, it was going to be by torch light at least. She dug her phone out of her pocket and was relieved to see it still had plenty of charge. A quick swipe of the screen and she had the phone's light on, ready to guide them. Benji looked down at the phone and then at Isla and smiled.

"Ok then, let's go. Follow me," said Benji as he disappeared down the hole.

Isla nervously followed, staying close behind Benji and using the phone's torch to light the way. Once Isla had climbed down the hole, she found herself in a maze of tunnels. They were big enough so that she could stand up without having to crouch down. They were like rabbit warrens but for elves.

"This way," said Benji as he disappeared down one of the many tunnels.

Benji certainly knew his way through the tunnels. He turned left and right, never hesitating once as to which way to go or which tunnel to take. He was right about the goblins not being able to follow them as there were that many different routes. Isla could imagine easily getting stuck down here forever if you didn't know where you were going.

It reminded her of the maze at the local adventure park she sometimes visited, although that was outside and made from large hedges instead of being deep underground surrounded by mud and almost in total darkness.

Eventually, much to Isla's relief, she saw daylight up ahead: sunlight shining through a small gap at the end of one of the tunnels. Benji crawled out the gap with ease, although it was a slightly tighter squeeze for Isla, but she managed it without getting stuck or too dirty. Once she was out, she brushed herself down and then took a look around at her new surroundings. She found herself in a large meadow that was covered in pretty yellow flowers similar in appearance to buttercups.

Isla scanned the vast meadow; she didn't know how far they had travelled through the tunnels, but she couldn't see the elves' settlement anywhere in the distance, and there was no sign of any goblins so, for now, it seemed they were safe.

"Where are we?" asked Isla

"This is the golden meadow; my friend Sophie lives just up there," said Benji pointing off into the distance.

Isla looked in the direction that Benji was pointing, and far away, she could just make out a small hut.

"We need to get to the chief high wizard's temple before Ivana and Barry get there and warn her about their plans," said Isla

"Barry, who on Atalan is Barry?" asked a rather confused-looking Benji.

"Barry is Warlock the sorcerer's real name," said Isla.

"Oh, I see, well that makes sense. If I was a wizard, I think I would rather be called Warlock than Barry," chuckled Benji.

"Anyway, which way is it to the temple, and how far away is it?" asked Isla.

"Umm, I've no idea. I have never been there. I thought you had?" said Benji.

"Well, yes, I have, but I teleported there so I have no idea how to get there or where it is," said Isla.

"Teleported, woo that sounds cool. Can't we just teleport back then?" asked Benji.

Isla shook her head and sighed.

"No, unfortunately not. The teleportation potion is in Steve's rucksack which Ivana now has. Without that we can't teleport, and I can't get home either," said Isla, looking sad.

"Well, maybe Sophie will be in. We could go and ask her if she knows how to get to the temple," said Benji with a smile.

"Do you think she will be able to help?" asked Isla.

"Well, she's a Bushwhacker, and they are pretty smart. Come on, let's go and see if she's in," said Benji as he set off through the golden meadow towards the hut in the distance.

As they walked along a well-trodden path that cut through the yellow flowers towards the hut, Benji asked Isla a barrage of questions all about Earth. Where did she live, how had she got to Atalan, what sort of foods did she eat, were the Avengers real? He asked so many questions in quick succession that Isla was finding it difficult to answer them all.

After what felt like the hundredth question, the pair reached the hut. It wasn't much to look at, and Isla was a little surprised that anyone could actually live in it. The hut was only slightly bigger than the shed in Isla's garden. It was made of wood with a roof that appeared to be built with a mixture of twigs and straw. There was a single door at the front and one window that you couldn't see through because of all the dust and cobwebs that covered it.

As they walked towards the front door, there was a rustling in the flowers from Isla's left. As she turned her head to see what had caused it, a group of small creatures walked out in front of them and moved very slowly across their path. Isla froze, not knowing what they were and if they were dangerous or not. The creatures had green spikey shells on their backs similar to a tortoise, and under the shells were four brown furry legs. Short and stumpy, the legs looked like they were struggling to carry the weight of the shell. Sticking out the front was a huge fluffy head that reminded Isla of monkeys and looked far too big for both the shell and the legs.

"What are they?" asked Isla as she counted eight of the creatures. They were easy to count as they moved at a snail's pace.

"Those are slothbottoms. The Bushwhackers love to keep them as pets and enjoy racing them," said Benji.

"Race them?" exclaimed Isla, "are they racing now?" she asked, laughing.

"Ha-ha, no not now as they haven't got their numbers on. They must just be training," said Benji as he stepped around the slothbottoms and walked up to the front door of the hut.

Before he had chance to knock, the door flew open and a girl who looked to be a similar age to Isla came flying out.

"Benjiiii boy!! What are you doing here? We haven't got a play date arranged, have we?" said the girl as she wrapped her arms around Benji, almost knocking his hat off in the process.

The girl had brown hair, which was tied back in a ponytail, along with big brown eyes. She was wearing a grey vest top with grey and black camo cargo trousers and black walking boots and was obviously very pleased to see Benji.

"Hey, Sophie, no we haven't got a play date arranged today, but we are in need of your help," said Benji as he freed himself from Sophie's grip.

"Hey, who's your friend?" asked Sophie as she spotted Isla stood behind Benji.

"This is Isla. She is from..." before Benji had chance to finish his sentence, Sophie interrupted.

"No way, this isn't Isla the Earth girl, is it?" as Sophie spoke, she bounded over to Isla and held her hand up for a high-five.

Isla blushed and nodded before high-fiving Sophie. How do so many people know about my previous visit to Atalan? Thought Isla.

"We have learnt about you in Bushwhacker school as part of our Bushwhacker trials. You are a bit of a hero of mine," said Sophie, beaming from ear to ear.

"Thank you," said Isla, feeling a little bit overwhelmed. She had never been someone's hero before.

"In fact, I have the book that was written about your adventures. You will have to sign it for me. That would be so cool."

"A book?!" said Isla, a little shocked.

"Yeah, it's a bestseller here in Atalan," said Sophie

Isla blushed; she couldn't believe she was now the main character of a book.

"So, how can I help you two?" asked Sophie.

Isla and Benji then proceeded to tell Sophie about everything that happened so far. Sophie stood in silence and listened intently until Isla had finished telling the story.

"Wow, it almost sounds made up, like a children's fantasy fiction story," said Sophie.

"So, what we really need is to get to the chief high wizard's temple and warn her about the plan to overthrow her," said Isla.

"Well, yes, that does sound like the best course of action," said Sophie.

"So, can you help?" asked Isla hopefully.

"That I cannot," answered Sophie.

Isla's heart sank. If Sophie couldn't help them, she really didn't know what else to do. She still had the serum but had no idea what to do with it, and now it appeared she was once again stranded on Atalan with no idea where she was or who could help.

"I mean, I would love to help," continued Sophie, "it's just that I don't know where the chief high wizard's temple is. We haven't been taught that yet in Bushwhacker school. Is there any other way I can help?"

Isla stood in silence for a moment trying her hardest to think of any other options. Maybe, just maybe, she could somehow use the serum to break the spell that the Unkerdunkies were under, and then with their help, they could free Wally. It was a long shot, but she didn't really have any other ideas.

"Do you know where the Unkerdunkies' village is?" asked Isla hopefully.

"I certainly do," said Sophie with a big smile.

"How far away is it, and could you take us there?" asked Isla.

"It's pretty far away, but we can ride on one of my pets to get us there quicker," said Sophie.

Isla looked down at a couple of slothbottoms that had only just overtaken Benji and were very slowly walking towards the front door.

"Do you mean ride on them?" asked Isla, pointing to the very sluggish creatures. Surely, walking would be much quicker than riding on of those she thought.

"Ha-ha no, not my slothbottoms," laughed Sophie.

She put a couple of fingers into her mouth and whistled. As the sound filled the air, the floor started to rumble, and the little hut started to shake. From behind Sophie's house, appeared a creature that Isla was very familiar with.

"A BUZZAGON," shouted Isla.

The last time she had encountered one of these beasts she had been sliding down an icy slope on a branch, with one hot on her tail, breathing fire. The buzzagon that had appeared in front of her was slightly smaller than she remembered the last one being, although it was still bigger than Sophie's hut.

It must have been lying down behind the house, which was why Isla hadn't seen it until now. And now it was far too close for comfort and getting closer by the second as it walked towards Isla, the floor shaking with its every step.

As Isla back-peddled away from the approaching buzzagon, she realised that Benji and Sophie hadn't moved a muscle; they hadn't reacted in any way. Almost as if the sight of one of these scary creatures was a common occurrence.

"Don't be scared, Isla, this is Buzzby. He's my pet buzzagon," said Sophie.

As she spoke, she held out her hand and made a clicking noise which Buzzby immediately reacted to. He walked over to Sophie and lowered his giant head so she could stroke him. As she ruffled his feathers, he let out a purring sound similar to that of a content cat.

"He's your pet?" said Isla, still keeping her distance from something that breathed fire and had sharp teeth and razor-like claws.

"Yes, we've had him since he was young. I found him near Snowy Point with an injured wing, and I brought him back here and nursed him back to health. He has stayed with us ever since," said Sophie as she gave Buzzby an affectionate rub.

This close up, Isla could see just how beautiful these creatures were when they were not chasing you and trying to set you on fire. Buzzby had green scaly skin with a spikey green tail that swished along the grass as Sophie petted him. His two giant wings were covered in bright blue and green feathers, and the claws on his feet were each the size of one of Isla's hands.

"So, what's the plan, Isla?" asked Benji.

"If we can't get to the temple, then I think our only option is to go to the Unkerdunkie village and somehow try and use this serum to break the spell that Barry has cast and set the Unkerdunkies and Wally free. If anyone will know how to put a stop to this, it will be Wally," said Isla.

"Do you think the Unkerdunkies can help us? And can we trust them?" asked Benji.

Isla sensed that there was maybe more than just a little friendly rivalry between the elves and the Unkerdunkies, but she didn't have time to worry about that. If they wanted to stop Ivana, Barry and

70

his goblin army from taking over Atalan, then they would all have to work together.

"Yes, we can trust them. They helped me before, and I'm sure they can help us again," said Isla.

"Well, it sounds like a plan to me. I will go and get Buzzby saddled up and ready to go," said Sophie, disappearing inside the hut.

Moments later, she reappeared carrying what looked like a large horse's saddle and reins. She placed the saddle on Buzzby' s back and fastened it tightly under his belly with a large metal clasp and then placed the reins over his head without any fuss from Buzzby.

"Will we all fit on there?" asked Isla.

"Yes, of course, this is a three-seater," said Sophie, patting the saddle as she spoke.

"Do you need to tell your folks you are going?" asked Benji.

"Nah, everyone has gone away for a few days. Ma and Pa took them all to the seaside to try and catch some blunder fish," said Sophie.

"They've taken everyone with them? Even little Jessy and Fredrick?" asked Benji.

"Yup," replied Sophie.

"Ralph and Bunny?" asked Benji.

"Yeah," said Sophie nodding.

"Surely, Margo and Tabby haven't gone? I thought they hated the water?" said Benji.

"Yeah, everyone went."

"How many people live here?" asked Isla.

"Well, there is Ma and Pa, Granny and Grandpops, and me and my 15 brothers and sisters. So, 20 of us in total," said Sophie.

Isla was a little surprised to say the least. One, by the fact that Sophie was one of 16 children, and also by the fact that 20 people could live in this hut. Maybe all the houses in Atalan were like this: small from the outside and then huge on the inside, similar to how Wally's house was, she thought to herself.

"Why didn't you go? I thought you loved it by the sea?" asked Benji.

"I stayed behind so I could train my slothbottoms. It's the big race in a few weeks, the Impressive Domestic Cup and Crimson Daiquiri has a great chance of winning it," said Sophie.

As she spoke, she bent down and stroked one of the slothbottoms who had given up the attempt to reach the hut and had collapsed in a heap on the floor. Isla guessed this must have been Crimson Daiquiri.

"Right, if we are ready, shall we go?" said Sophie.

Sophie made another clicking sound, and on command, Buzzby laid down so that Sophie could easily climb onto the saddle and take the reins. Benji went next and sat in the middle, holding onto Sophie, and Isla took the rear. She clung onto Benji as tightly as she could. It reminded her of being on

72

the branch and holding onto Fartybubble for dear life, only that time she was escaping from a buzzagon instead of about to ride one.

"If we are all on, then let's go. Hold on tight," shouted Sophie.

With a tap of her feet and a gentle pull on the reins, Buzzby rose up and extended his large wings and began to flap them. He lifted off the floor, and within seconds, they were soaring high above the ground and leaving the meadow far behind them.

Chapter 7

The moment Buzzby left the ground, Isla shut her eyes tightly and held onto Benji for dear life. As the buzzagon climbed higher into the sky, Isla felt her stomach starting to churn. It was the feeling she got when she went on a rollercoaster, usually at the moment the ride reached the top of its assent before plummeting back down to earth. She hoped that there would be no plummeting today.

After a few seconds, Sophie pulled gently on the reins, and Buzzby stopped climbing. He spread out his wings and glided gracefully through the air.

"Wow, the view is amazing," shouted Benji.

Isla dared to open an eye, followed slowly by the other. Benji was right, the view was indeed amazing. From their vantage point high up in the clouds, Isla could see the beautiful Atalan landscape unfolding below. They passed over luscious green fields, densely covered forests, valleys and mountains.

Isla was starting to relax and actually enjoy the ride, with the wind in her hair and the sound of Buzzby gently flapping his wings as he soared majestically through the blue sky. The only slight irritation was the occasional bobble in her face from Benji's hat as it blew in the breeze.

As they flew on, Isla noticed the landscape below suddenly change. The luscious greens became a covering of white snow as they passed over Snowy Point. They were now in an area of Atalan that she knew, and memories of her previous visit started to come flooding back. She recalled the snowball fight she had with Fartybubble and Oliver, and the image of Fartybubble lying flat on his back in the snow after a direct hit came into her head and brought a smile to her face.

They passed through Snowy Point, and once again, the landscape changed to an orchard filled with trees covered in bright red berries.

"Frothing berries," said Isla quietly to herself.

She recalled the sweet taste of the berries and the burping and floating that they caused. Isla found herself chuckling as she pictured Fartybubble floating up into the sky after licking berry juice off his face after mistaking it for blood.

After passing the orchard, the ground below became a mass of trees as they swooped over Forest Glades. They were getting closer to the Unkerdunkie village.

"The village isn't far away. Where do you want me to land?" Sophie shouted to Isla, trying to make herself heard over the wind.

"Anywhere you can but just a little away from the village as we don't want the goblins to see us arrive," shouted Isla.

Sophie nodded and then gently pulled on the reins causing Buzzby to roll to his right before he started descending towards the tops of the trees. Isla wasn't sure where Sophie was aiming for as there didn't seem to be any gaps amongst the dense forest canopy for a buzzagon and three passengers to fit through!

As the treetops got alarmingly closer by the second, Isla once again closed her eyes tightly and hung onto Benji, bracing herself for impact. She felt Buzzby veer to his left slightly, and the next second, she could feel leaves and branches brushing through her hair and against her body, followed by a slight thud and a shudder as the buzzagon's two giant feet came into contact with the forest floor and Buzzby came to a halt after an almost near perfect landing.

"What a rush, that was sick," shouted a very excited Benji.

Isla opened her eyes and gave herself a quick examination. Apart from a few twigs and leaves in her hair, she was perfectly fine with not even a scratch on her. She slowly and carefully climbed down from Buzzby and scanned the area. It appeared they had landed a little bit away from the Unkerdunkies' village and more importantly out of sight of any goblins.

"So, what's the plan now? Shall we just charge the village and let Buzzby do his thing with his flames?" said Benji.

"No, we can't do that because the Unkerdunkies are there, and they might get hurt," said Isla.

"Can't we?" asked Benji.

Isla shot the little elf a look.

"I mean no, we can't," said Benji sheepishly.

"We can't go charging in there while the Unkerdunkies are under the goblins' command as they might be forced to fight us, and we don't want them getting injured. I suggest we try and find a way of getting the Unkerdunkies to drink this serum, and then, hopefully, we can get them away to safety before we unleash Buzzby," said Isla.

"Sounds like a good idea to me. I will leave Buzzby here for the time being to rest," said Sophie.

She tethered his reins to a branch of a nearby tree and gave him a stroke.

"We won't be long, boy," said Sophie.

Buzzby once again lowered his head so he could be fussed and purred happily.

Isla watched this big scary-looking creature purring contently and licking Sophie's hand as she tickled him under his chin. While he certainly looked menacing and the sight of him alone might scare some of the goblins away, Isla was worried that if any of them did put up a fight, the only thing Buzzby would do was roll on his back to have his tummy tickled.

"Do you think Buzzby will breathe fire at the goblins?" Isla asked Sophie.

"He will if I give him the command," said Sophie with a big smile.

"Ok great, let's head towards the village then as quietly as we can. We don't want to be spotted by any goblins," said Isla.

The trio moved through the forest as silently as they could, constantly scanning the area for any goblins. They reached the edge of the village without any trouble and took cover behind a large tree. The scene in front of Isla was very similar to how it had been when she was previously here with Steve, although there did appear to be slightly less goblins around this time. Maybe some of them are the ones who are invading the elves' settlement with Barry, Isla thought.

Isla pulled out the bottle of serum that she had safely stashed in her jeans pocket and held it up to her face to study it. Apart from the label that said SER on it, there were no other writing or markings. Certainly no directions on how to use it, that was for sure. How Isla was going to get all the Unkerdunkies to drink this clear liquid was beyond her. She wasn't even sure if drinking it was the way to administer the serum, and if it was, how much did you have to drink for it to work?!

Isla watched the scene inside the village, desperately hoping for a brain wave and a great idea to pop into her head. She watched the Unkerdunkies bringing the baskets of fruit and the big buckets of water that were being poured into the trough. She saw a couple of Unkerdunkies cooking a meal for the goblins in a large pot over an open fire, and she even saw one entertaining a group of them by doing backflips and cartwheels. She watched as the little Unkerdunkie finished his last flip before walking over to the trough and downing a large cup of water before he was ordered back to do some more acrobatics.

It was at that moment as if a light bulb had gone off in Isla's head: of course, the water trough. Not only were the goblins drinking out of it but so were the Unkerdunkies. If she could pour the serum into there, then maybe they would all drink it and the spell would be broken.

Isla quickly outlined her plan to Benji and Sophie and both of them nodded enthusiastically and agreed it was a good idea, although this could have been due to the fact that neither of them had any other plans.

"I just need to get across to that trough without getting spotted," said Isla.

The water trough stood behind a large tree on the opposite side of a small clearing. There were a number of goblins lying around between Isla and her intended target, and she would need some kind of distraction to make it across unseen.

"I have a wicked idea," whispered Benji with a big grin on his face.

Before Isla had chance to ask what it was, Benji was up and darting away to his right before disappearing behind a cluster of large bushes. A few moments later, Isla heard a strange sound coming from that direction. It sounded like someone doing a bad impression of an owl.

"What's he doing?" Isla said, whispering to Sophie.

"He's making the sound of a conkaburrow. It's actually quite a good impression," said Sophie.

"But why?" asked Isla.

"Because conkaburrows are very dangerous. One sting from them can be deadly," said Sophie.

As Benji continued with his owl in pain kind of sound, Isla noticed activity in the village. The goblins who had been lying down watching the Unkerdunkie doing his flips and cartwheels were suddenly jumping to their feet and grabbing their weapons. There seemed to be a bit of panic amongst the goblins as they started shouting and pointing in the direction the strange sound was coming from. Instead of going to investigate it themselves though, they started ordering a couple of Unkerdunkies to go and check it out.

This distraction was all that Isla needed. With the goblins' attention drawn away from the direction of the water trough, Isla made her move. She raced across the clearing as quickly as possible staying as low as she could. When she reached the trough, she threw herself behind it and stayed hidden for a few moments.

Eventually, Isla peered out over the top of the trough and surveyed the scene. The Unkerdunkies who had been sent to check out the potential conkaburrow were now heading back from the bushes. Luckily, they obviously hadn't found Benji and now that the sound had stopped, the goblins seemed happy to go back to what they were doing.

Isla undid the top of the serum bottle and held it over the water trough. She hesitated for a second not knowing if what she was about to do would even work, before she carefully poured a drop into the water. There was a slight plop as the two liquids met, but apart from that, nothing else happened. The drinking water didn't change colour; there was no fizzing or smoke or anything.

Isla looked at the serum bottle. She had only put a tiny amount in so far, and she really didn't know if that was enough or not. She looked around the village at the amount of Unkerdunkies that were here and decided she needed to pour more in. She looked at the serum once more and then shrugged her shoulders before tipping the rest in. She left a tiny amount in the bottle just in case she might need it later.

Once it was done, Isla crouched down behind the large tree and waited, hoping that an Unkerdunkie would be along soon to take a drink. Luckily, she didn't have to wait long before one arrived at the trough. He had been carrying a bucket of water which he had emptied into the trough before grabbing a cup and filling it to the top. He downed his drink before taking his hat off so he could wipe the sweat off his brow. His brown hair was flat to his head and ringing wet, the sweat running down his cheeks and into his bushy brown beard. It was because of this mass of facial hair that Isla hadn't recognised the Unkerdunkie at first, but as she looked on, the penny dropped.

"Fartybubble," whispered Isla.

Unfortunately, Isla whispered slightly too loud and Fartybubble heard it, his eyes fixing on hers. He stared straight at her, dropping his cup in surprise. Isla held her breath and remained completely still. Had the serum worked? Would Fartybubble raise the alarm or try and capture her and would he even recognise Isla after all this time?

For a moment, there was complete silence. Fartybubble looked at Isla then around the village and then back at Isla. A confused look spread across his face.

"Isla, is that you?" he said very slowly.

Isla could have jumped with joy but she resisted, she couldn't afford to be spotted by the goblins. Instead, she gave Fartybubble the world's biggest smile and beckoned him over.

"Isla, what are you doing here, and why are there goblins in the village?" said Fartybubble as he joined Isla behind the tree.

Before Isla answered, she threw her arms around Fartybubble and gave him a big hug. It was so nice to see a familiar face.

"Fartybubble, I am so glad to see you. Now, we haven't got much time, and it's quite a long story, so I'm going to keep it as short as possible. The Unkerdunkies have been put under a spell by an evil wizard who is being helped by the goblins. You are being made to do everything the goblins tell you. I've managed to get hold of a serum which will break the spell, and I have poured it into the water trough. When you drink the water like you just have, the spell will wear off. I need you to get all the Unkerdunkies to drink from that trough and then get them away to safety. Do you understand?" said Isla.

Fartybubble shook his head. He looked completely bewildered.

"Just go and tell all the other Unkerdunkies to come and get a drink. Can you do that?" asked Isla.

Very slowly, Fartybubble nodded his head.

"Ok great. Try and act natural, and if any of the goblins ask you to do something, you have to do it, ok?" asked Isla.

"Ok," said Fartybubble.

He got up and retrieved his bucket and then headed off towards a group of Unkerdunkies. Isla watched him he go. He kept his head down and tried to avoid any eye contact with the goblins. Each time he came to a fellow Unkerdunkie, he would whisper in their ear and usher them in the direction of the water trough. Slowly one by one they would head over to the trough and take a drink.

"It's working," Isla whispered to herself.

Each time an Unkerdunkie would take a drink of water the same thing happened: at first they seemed a little confused, then they would look around the village and see it was filled with goblins, and the look of confusion would turn to fear. Isla would then get their attention and beckon them over to her hiding place behind the large tree. She would explain as quickly as possible what was going on before sending the Unkerdunkie back out into the village to direct more of their friends over to drink the water.

Soon there was a large line of Unkerdunkies queuing up by the water trough with cups in their hands, wondering why it was so urgent that they have a drink. Unfortunately, this attracted the attention of some of the goblins, and a couple of them started shouting over to the Unkerdunkies. Isla couldn't understand what was being said, but it seemed like the goblins were demanding that the Unkerdunkies went back to whatever jobs they had been doing, immediately. When the Unkerdunkies, who had already drunk the serum refused to budge, the goblins became even angrier and started approaching the water trough with their weapons drawn.

Isla peeked out from behind the tree and saw the goblins advancing towards her hiding place. At the sight of the angry goblins coming towards them, the Unkerdunkies who had already drank from the trough reacted by making a run for it. Some of them jumped onto nearby wooden platforms that were suspended from the trees by large ropes that were used by the Unkerdunkies as lifts to reach their tree houses above. Others made a dash for the trees and disappeared into the forest. The Unkerdunkies who had yet to drink the serum-infused water stood around looking puzzled at what was going on.

At the sight of so many Unkerdunkies trying to escape, the rest of the goblins reacted. They stopped whatever they had been doing and grabbed their weapons and started giving chase. Isla watched as complete pandemonium took over the village. Goblins and Unkerdunkies ran around all over the place like a giant game of tag had started.

Suddenly, a huge roar came from the forest followed by the sight of Buzzby coming through the trees ridden by Sophie and Benji. The cavalry has arrived, thought Isla.

The appearance of a large fire-breathing buzzagon sent panic through the village. Unkerdunkies ran for cover as well as a few of the goblins who dropped their weapons and turned and fled. A brave bunch of goblins stood their ground with their weapons drawn, but rather than try and take on the beast themselves, they commended the Unkerdunkies to go and fight it. Even the Unkerdunkies who had yet to drink the serum and were still under the goblins' spell were having none of that, spell or no spell they were not about to take on an angry buzzagon.

Realising the Unkerdunkies were not going to help them, the goblins decided to try and drive the buzzagon back themselves. They approached Buzzby, waving their staffs towards him. At the sight of this and on Sophie's command, Buzzby let out a burst of fire which set alight the forest floor just in front of the goblins, almost singeing their toes.

That was all it took for the goblins to turn on their heels and flee, leaving the Unkerdunkie village far behind them.

Isla watched them disappear into the forest before she came out from behind the tree and into the clearing. She began shouting for the Unkerdunkies to come out from their hiding places, telling them that it was now safe to do so. She called out for Fartybubble and Oliver as she searched the village trying to find her two friends.

After a few moments, Isla spotted Oliver. He was stood over towards the water trough, his eyes were glazed over, and he had an expressionless look on his face. It appeared he had not yet drunk the water that contained the serum. Isla raced over to him.

"Oliver, are you ok?" said Isla.

Oliver stared back at her blankly. It appeared he didn't recognise her or have any idea what was going on.

"Here, drink this, it will make you feel better," said Isla, grabbing a cup and filling it from the trough.

Oliver took a big gulp of the drink, and a few seconds later, the serum kicked in.

"Isla, what are you doing here. What is going on?" said Oliver.

Before Isla had chance to answer, Fartybubble appeared from behind a tree that he had taken cover behind and came rushing over.

"I don't want to alarm anyone, but what is that doing in our village?" a very scared Fartybubble said, pointing towards the buzzagon that was now standing in the middle of the clearing.

"Yes, what is THAT doing here?" said Oliver, pointing in the same direction.

"Don't be scared, that's Buzzby, and he's friendly. He's a pet of Sophie's, who is a Bushwhacker who has been helping me," said Isla.

"I didn't mean the buzzagon, I meant the elf," said Oliver with a look of disgust on his face.

As Oliver spoke, Benji jumped down off Buzzby and walked over.

"Nice outfit!" said Benji to Oliver with a very large hint of sarcasm.

"Have you come to our village because not only do you dress like us you also want to be like us?" replied Oliver.

What followed was a few minutes of childish bickering, covering such topics as who had the best clothes, the biggest house and the largest hat. Eventually, Isla had enough of it.

"Can you two stop arguing?! There are more important things to worry about at this moment in time than who has got the biggest hat. The goblins and Barry are trying to take over Atalan, and if they succeed, you will be put under their spell and forced to do whatever it is they tell you to. Your life will not be your own. Also, if that happens, I will be stranded here and will never get home to see my family again. If we are to stop them, we all need to work together," said Isla.

As she spoke, her eyes began to fill with tears. She had managed to put the thought of not getting home to the back of her mind while she focused on trying to rescue the Unkerdunkies. Now, though, the realisation that she may be stuck here once again set in.

"Well said, young Isla," came a voice from behind her.

She turned around to see Wally stepping off a lift that had brought him down from high up in the trees where he had been held prisoner. In all the commotion he had managed to escape from the makeshift cell.

"Wally," shouted Isla.

She raced over to him and threw her arms around the wizard. She was so pleased to see him. If anyone would know how to stop Barry and Ivana, it would be Wally.

"It is great to see you again, Isla, but where is Steve? I thought he would be coming to rescue me?" asked Wally.

Isla then began to explain exactly what had been going on so far and how they desperately needed some help. She introduced Sophie and Benji to Wally and the rest of the Unkerdunkies, who by now had all drunk the water and were no longer under the spell.

Once Isla had finished telling her story, Oliver sheepishly held his hand out to Benji.

"Isla is right, we are all in this together. I'm sorry for what I said. Thank you for helping Isla rescue us, and I hope we can repay the favour and help you free your family," said Oliver.

Benji smiled and nodded before shaking Oliver's hand.

"I'm sorry as well. Any help in freeing my family would be greatly appreciated," said Benji.

"You two must be thirsty. How about me and my bro take you up into our village and get you some of our famous sagar berry juice," said Oliver gesturing towards Benji and Sophie.

"That would be lovely, thank you," replied Sophie.

"Yes, thank you, although I'm sure it won't be as nice as the elves' pimple berry pop," said Benji with a chuckle.

And with that the two Unkerdunkies led Sophie and Benji away to get them a drink, laughing and joking as they went.

"What is it with elves and Unkerdunkies?" Isla asked Wally as she watched the four climb onto a lift and disappear up into the trees.

"Well, it's a rivalry that is passed down from generation to generation. In Atalan, we play a game which uses a dried Merrybell berry. The berry is large and round and two teams kick it up and down a field trying to get it between two posts either end of the pitch," said Wally.

"Like football?" asked Isla.

"A bit like football although that is only a sport, nothing more than just a game that you play. Kicksphere is much more than that. The rivalries are much fiercer. Entire races almost go to war, families fall out and even friends become enemies, depending which team they support," said Wally.

"Yep, sounds like football," said Isla.

"Each year all the teams from the area compete for the Atalan cup and both the elves and the Unkerdunkies take part. They are the two best teams in the whole of Atalan, and for the last ten years, they have met each other in the final. The elves have won the cup for the past three years, so as you can imagine, the Unkerdunkies are not happy about it," said Wally.

"I see," said Isla.

While the thought of entire races falling out over a simple game baffled Isla, she sort of understood it. She remembered back to the time the football world cup was on and how animated her dad had got every time England had played. She had never seen her dad get as upset as he had the time England had been knocked out in a penalty shoot-out. Her mum telling him that it was only a game had certainly not helped!

After the brief history of the rivalry between the elves and the Unkerdunkies, Isla asked Wally about what had happened to him and how he had ended up in a wooden cage high up in the trees.

Wally explained how Barry along with Fizzbit, who was already under the spell, and the goblins had arrived at his house and had kicked the door down and had taken him captive before he had a chance to defend himself. The only thing he had time to do was to hide the serum under the floor in the hope that Steve or someone else would find it. The goblins had ransacked his house and had taken away all of his potions and his wand, but luckily they never discovered the serum.

After that, he was taken away and led to the Unkerdunkie village where, on their arrival, Barry had cast his spell and put the entire village under his command. Once that had happened, Wally explained how he was held prisoner inside the cage while Barry, Fizzbit and a small army of goblins had left to go and invade the elves' settlement.

Suddenly, Wally's story was interrupted by shouting from above. Surely, Oliver and Benji haven't fallen out already, thought Isla?! She looked up to see Oliver, Fartybubble, and their two newfound friends racing back down to the forest floor on the lift. They were waving their arms around frantically, pointing towards something in the distance. It was difficult to hear what they were yelling about as all four of them were shouting at the same time.

Both Isla and Wally turned to look in the direction the foursome were pointing and immediately saw what was causing all the commotion. Coming through the forest in the distance was another group of goblins, only this time they were not alone. Leading the pack was Fizzbit, and the giant troll didn't look happy.

Chapter 8

Sophie and Benji jumped off the lift first onto the forest floor and sprinted across the ground over to where Buzzby was. The gentle beast had found a spot in the sun and was lying on his side soaking up the rays. A few of the Unkerdunkies had found the courage to come over and stroke this giant creature that had come to their rescue and had helped drive the goblins away.

Sophie grabbed Buzzby's reins and made a few clicking noises which the buzzagon again reacted to, this time by rolling onto his belly. Once he had done this, Sophie jumped onto the saddle and gave the reins a gentle tug. Buzzby rose up onto his feet and spread out his wings and let out a roar. At the sight and sound of this, the nearby Unkerdunkies all jumped back.

"What are you doing?" asked Isla.

"Stopping that massive troll and the horde of goblins from taking over the village again," shouted Sophie.

Fizzbit had almost reached the clearing, and the sight of him had sent the Unkerdunkies running once more, back up the lifts they went, disappearing behind trees and hiding under bushes.

"You can't attack Fizzbit, he is a friend and nothing more than a gentle giant," shouted Isla.

While Fizzbit was obviously under Barry's spell, his face showing the same expressionless look as Oliver had before drinking the serum, Isla didn't want him being attacked by Buzzby. He was her friend and had helped her the last time she was here.

"He's under the spell though, Isla, and we need to stop him. I haven't got my wand, and I can't see a way you can get him to drink the serum," said Wally.

Isla looked towards the approaching troll and then to the bottle of serum she still held in her hand. There was a tiny drop left and just maybe that was all she needed. She had stood up to Fizzbit before when everyone else had thought he was a big scary troll, and she could do it again. Or at least she could try.

"Just stay here with Buzzby and don't move unless I tell you too. Please, Sophie," begged Isla.

Sophie looked down at Isla and reluctantly nodded.

"Isla, what are you going to do?" asked Wally.

"This," shouted Isla.

And with that, she was off, sprinting through the village towards the oncoming Fizzbit, her friends shouting from behind for her to stop and that it was too dangerous.

Isla stopped directly in front of Fizzbit, blocking his path into the village. Fizzbit though didn't stop or even slow down, he just continued his march forwards. If Isla didn't do anything quickly then the giant troll would simply step right over her, or even worse, onto her!

"Fizzbit, it's me, Isla. Don't you remember the girl from Earth who you helped get home? You let me across your bridge, and you helped rescue me from the goblins," shouted Isla.

Still no reaction from Fizzbit, his expression hadn't changed, not even a flinch. He just kept charging forwards.

"You are under a spell, Fizzbit, you are being made to help the goblins. Remember you don't even like the goblins, they are mean to you. They throw bottles at you," Isla shouted again, the panic starting to set in.

The troll just kept coming forwards while all the time being egged on by the goblins behind him.

"Fizzbit, drink this, and it will break the spell," screamed Isla as she tossed the bottle of serum towards him.

She held her breath as the bottle flew through the air towards Fizzbit's face. At the last moment before it was about to hit him, he raised a giant hand and caught the bottle. He looked down at this object that had been thrown at him, tiny in his hands, and then looked over at Isla.

"Please, Fizzbit, drink it," begged Isla.

The goblins were now shouting and screaming at Fizzbit, urging him to continue forwards and to trample over whoever was foolish enough to stand in his way.

Fizzbit turned and looked at the goblins and then back to Isla before finally looking at the bottle in his grasp. He knocked the bottle top clean off with just a flick of his finger and downed the last drop of serum.

Isla held her breath. Would such a small amount have any effect on a huge troll?

For a few moments, nothing happened, Fizzbit just stood in silence staring at Isla. He didn't say a word or move a muscle, he just remained completely still. The goblins looked on, unsure as to why this massive troll that was under their spell had frozen in front of a tiny girl.

Eventually, two of the goblins got tired of the inactivity and approached Fizzbit from either side. They were shouting and screaming at him, obviously in an attempt to make him carry on towards the village. When Fizzbit didn't move, they both raised their weapons and got ready to attack.

Without warning, Fizzbit raised both fists and slammed them into each of the goblins, literally knocking them clean off their feet and sending them flying backwards into the horde behind them. The goblins were sent scattering like skittles in a bowling alley.

Fizzbit turned around and approached the fallen goblins as they scrambled to their feet and tried to retrieve their weapons which were now littered all over the forest floor. The first one to his feet decided to charge at Fizzbit. He grabbed his long staff which had a large circular blade attached to one end that made him look like a lollipop man who you wouldn't want to cross!

He raced towards his intended target and raised his staff, but before he had chance to strike, Fizzbit simply reached out one of his massive arms and scooped up the weapon with the goblin still attached.

Fizzbit held the staff with the goblin still holding on for dear life in front of his face and smiled. The goblin was kicking and thrashing around like a fish on a hook, desperately trying to free the staff from the troll's giant fist.

"BOO," shouted Fizzbit.

This was all it took for the goblin to let go of his staff. He dropped to the floor and landed on his feet. As he turned to run away, he ran straight into the pack of goblins who were still picking themselves up from their previous knockdown.

Isla couldn't help but let out a chuckle at the sight of the goblins falling all over the place; it was like a scene from a slapstick comedy.

Fizzbit took the staff and snapped it like it was a toothpick and tossed it into the undergrowth. At the sight of the goblins clamouring to get back up in front of him, he too started laughing. Isla watched as Fizzbit's huge shoulders went up and down as the troll laughed uncontrollably to himself. His chuckle echoed all around the forest causing the nearby trees to shake.

Eventually, the goblins managed to get back onto their feet, grab their weapons and compose themselves. They turned to face Fizzbit with their weapons raised and readied themselves to attack as one. Fizzbit stopped laughing, and he clenched his enormous fists and held his arms out wide and let out a monstrous roar. The sound was deafening, and the entire forest seemed to shudder.

The goblins turned to run, and once again, they ran straight into each other, sending bodies crashing to the floor. In their haste to get up, they stepped on, tripped over and fell into each other. This was too much for both Isla and Fizzbit to take, and they both ended up bent double from laughing so much, with tears streaming down their cheeks.

Eventually, the goblins managed to drag themselves to their feet, and for the second time that day, they retreated from the Unkerdunkie village as quickly as they could.

Once Isla had managed to stop laughing, she raced over to Fizzbit and threw her arms around his legs.

"Fizzbit, I am so glad to see you," said Isla with a huge smile on her face.

"Isla, it is great to see you again, but what are you doing back in Atalan, and why was I with the goblins?" asked a slightly confused Fizzbit.

"I will explain everything," said Isla.

She reached up and wrapped a hand around one of his huge fingers and led him into the village.

As they arrived into the clearing, a huge cheer went up from the Unkerdunkies who had watched Isla break the spell on Fizzbit before he drove away the goblins.

Oliver and Fartybubble came rushing over to congratulate Isla on her bravery and to give Fizzbit a fist bump each. It was great to see their troll friend again especially now he wasn't under the spell of an evil wizard.

As well as Oliver and Fartybubble congratulating Isla, another familiar face came over to say well done to her. Thunderbum, the head of the village, had come down from his hut in the trees and had been given a cup of water to drink. With the spell now broken, he was keen to learn what had happened to him and his people.

With the spell now lifted on the entire village, Wally got all the Unkerdunkies to sit around in a circle so that he and Isla could explain to them what had been going on. It soon became clear that neither the Unkerdunkies nor Fizzbit had any recollection of what had happened to them. They could remember seeing the goblins and Barry arrive, but after that there was nothing. Wally explained that it was like being hypnotised and that they had been under their complete control until the spell had been broken, and after they would have no memory of what had happened.

"So, how do we put a stop to this?" asked Thunderbum.

"I need to get to the chief high wizard's temple as quickly as possible, before Barry and Ivana. Sophie, could you take me there on your buzzagon?" asked Wally.

"If you tell me the way, then I certainly can," said Sophie, jumping up from off the floor.

"I want to come as well. I need to find Steve and his teleportation spell so I can get home," said Isla.

"And I want to go and teach Barry a lesson for making me do his dirty work," said a very cross-looking Fizzbit.

"And I want to come and kick some Goblin butt!" shouted Oliver as he jumped up off the floor and threw his arms around as if shadow boxing.

"Sit down, son," ordered Thunderbum.

Oliver sheepishly sat back down onto the ground.

"Well, we can't all go to the temple. I suggest I go with Sophie and Benji on the buzzagon. Fizzbit, why don't you bring Isla with you? I'm sure you can cover the ground easily. Do you know the way to the temple?" said Wally.

Fizzbit nodded.

"I suggest everyone else stays here and protects the village just in case the goblins come back. Stay up in the trees out of the way, and you will be fine," said Wally.

"That sounds like a good plan to me. We wish you a safe journey, and hopefully we will see you soon after all this is over," said Thunderbum.

As Isla got ready to leave with Fizzbit, Oliver and Fartybubble came over to say their goodbyes.

"Stay safe, and I hope we get chance to have a proper catch up before you return to Earth," said Fartybubble.

"Go kick some goblin butt, and give that Barry a slap from me as well," said Oliver.

Once Isla had said her goodbyes, Fizzbit scooped her up onto his giant shoulders. Wally climbed up onto Buzzby and sat in the middle between Sophie and Benji.

"Are we all ready?" asked Wally.

He got nods from all round and a thumbs up from Fizzbit.

"We will see you at the temple. Have a safe journey," said Wally.

And with that, Sophie pulled the reins and gave a click to signal Buzzby to go. He flapped his wings and rose gracefully into the air before disappearing through the trees above.

"Are you ready?" Fizzbit asked Isla.

"Yes, I am," replied Isla.

"Hold on tight," said Fizzbit.

And with that he was off, running through the forest at lightning speed. He may not be able to fly, but at the speed in which he could cover the ground,

Isla had a feeling they might reach the temple before Buzzby.

Chapter 9

Ivana stood at the entrance to the temple with Barry to her right and a horde of 20 goblins behind her. In her right hand, she held her staff, and over her left shoulder, she carried Steve's rucksack.

Barry and the goblins had their hands held out in front of them with their wrists bound together by some sort of tape. To the unsuspecting eye, it looked like Ivana had captured them and was returning to the temple as a hero after saving the elves from the evil Warlock.

What had actually happened was that Ivana and Barry had placed the elves under their spell and had captured the settlement. Steve's brave efforts to stop Ivana had been thwarted, and she had easily overpowered him with her staffjitsu. He was now under lock and key in a makeshift cell back at the elves' settlement and guarded by the remaining goblins.

The elves had been put to work much like the Unkerdunkies had and were now busy fetching and carrying water, cooking food and being made to entertain their goblin captors. Ivana, Barry and the small army of goblins had teleported back to the temple using Steve's own potion, ready to carry out the next phase of their plan.

Ivana and her 'prisoners' were escorted through the temple by two of the wizard's assistants and were shown through to the throne room. On her arrival into the throne room, Ivana noticed that the chief high wizard wasn't sat on her throne; in fact, she wasn't anywhere to be seen.

The wizard's assistants were dotted around the room, obviously enjoying some down time while their boss wasn't there to keep an eye on them.

A couple of them were sat on the red carpet deep in conversation while Matilda and Noel were playing a game of pool. Matilda was contemplating a difficult shot as her blue ball was tucked behind another blue ball.

Another assistant was busy trying to set a new high score on the arcade machine and was extremely animated in doing so. He was banging the buttons and wiggling the joystick with so much force that it was a surprise that he hadn't toppled the machine over.

Over by the mirror, a couple of assistants were checking themselves out and preening their feathers in the reflection while another was sat on the throne using the chief's tablet. She was frantically swiping her finger left and right on a wizard dating app.

At the sight of Ivana and her prisoners, the assistants immediately stopped what they were doing and hurried back to their places either side of the red carpet and took up the guard of honour formation.

"Where is the chief?" asked Ivana.

Before any of the assistants had a chance to reply, the chief high wizard came hurrying into the throne room, puffing and panting.

"What perfect timing, Ivana. I've just finished a brutal spin session," said the chief as she walked gingerly across the room and over to her throne. She sat down and gave a little wince.

The chief was dressed in an all-white tracksuit with bright white trainers. Around her neck was the necklace, and her golden wand was pushed through her hair and being used as a hair pin to keep it up. She slid it out, letting her hair fall down over her shoulders, and placed it on the arm of the throne.

Her face was red, and her forehead glistened with sweat as she mopped her brow with a towel that was just as white as the rest of her outfit.

"Congratulations, Ivana, I see you were successful in your mission," said the chief, looking over towards Barry.

Ivana walked down the red carpet past the wizard's assistants and stopped just in front of the steps that led up to the small platform that the throne stood on, and did the customary bow, curtsy combination.

"Yes, I had no problem in stopping Warlock and his goblin army and saving Atalan from their fiendish plans," said Ivana with a smile.

The chief high wizard nodded her approval before turning to Barry.

"Did you really think you would get away with this? You should have stayed banished," said the chief.

Barry didn't reply; instead, he just shrugged his shoulders.

"Where are Steve and the Earth girl? And what happened to the troll and the rest of the goblin army?" asked the chief as she looked around the room.

"Once I had broken the spell that Warlock had cast on the troll, I let him go. He has returned back to his bridge where he belongs. The rest of the goblin army I banished back to their kingdom as you requested. I brought these back with me so that you could give them a personal telling off before you place them all under house arrest," said Ivana as she pointed to the 20 goblins who stood in a line behind her.

"And Steve and Isla?" asked the chief.

"They decided they needed to return to Earth right away, so they have teleported back. Steve sends his regards and thanks you for all your help, Your Wizardness," lied Ivana.

"Ah, I see, well that's a shame. I was looking forward to seeing him before he left," said the chief.

As she spoke, she noticed the rucksack that Ivana was carrying over her left shoulder.

"Isn't that Steve's bag? Doesn't he need it?" asked the chief.

"Not where he is going," said Ivana with a menacing laugh.

The chief gave her a puzzled look but thought nothing more of the comment and instead she turned her attention back to Barry.

"So, Warlock, before I send you down to the temple prison, where you will spend the rest of your days, just tell me one thing. Why did you do it?" asked the chief.

"Because I want to rule Atalan," replied Barry.

"Well, luckily for us that is never going to happen," said the chief, smiling.

"That's what you think," said Barry with a chuckle.

As the words left his mouth, the goblins sprang into action. They ripped the loose-fitting tape off their wrists that had supposedly been restraining them and attacked the wizard's assistants. They knocked the staffs out of their hands before the assistants had a chance to unleash their powers, and outnumbering them, they were easily able to tackle them to the floor where they pinned them to the ground.

The moment the goblins attacked, so did Ivana. She swung her staff and knocked the chief high wizard's golden wand off the arm of the throne and onto the floor where it rolled across the tiles and out of her reach. Before the chief had a chance to react, Barry had also ripped the tape from his hands and had made a lunge for her necklace. He tore it from her, snapping the chain in the process.

"What on Atalan!" screamed the chief.

Ivana raced over to the golden wand that was lying on the ground and picked it up before tossing it over to Barry. He caught it in his left hand while holding the necklace in his right.

"Do not move," shouted Barry as he pointed the wand towards the stunned chief.

The chief high wizard sat on her throne looking shell-shocked, her face now as white as her tracksuit. She looked at Barry and then over to Ivana.

"Why, Ivana, why would you do such a thing? You were my most loyal assistant," said the chief, her voice shaking as she spoke.

"For power, of course. You have ruled Atalan for long enough, and now it's time for a change," said Ivana.

"And what do you plan to do with those?" asked the chief as she turned back to Barry and pointed to the golden wand and necklace that he now held.

"Do you think I'm going to tell you my master plan like they do in the movies just so you can then escape and stop me?" laughed Barry.

The chief high wizard just held out her arms and shrugged her shoulders.

"Ok then, I will tell you. I am going to go to the highest point of Volcano Mountain and find the mystical stone of Atalan. Legend says that when the stone is inserted into the necklace owned by the chief high wizard then the wearer will have the ultimate power and will be able to control the whole of Atalan. As well as that, I will be able to open dimensions to other worlds. I will be able to take over the universe, the multiverse and any other verse you can think of!" said Barry as he let out his best evil villain laugh that he could muster.

"We," said Ivana, quickly correcting Barry.

"Oh yes, I mean we, we will be able to take over the universe," said Barry.

"You will never get away with this," shouted the chief towards Barry.

"WE will never get away with it, you mean," said Ivana who was starting to get a little frustrated.

"And who is going to stop me? The only thing you have at your disposal now is a towel, and I know that isn't one of your magic ones because you don't use them for the gym," said Barry pointing to the white gym towel the chief was still holding.

"STOP US," screamed Ivana, her face becoming almost as red as her hair.

"Without your wand and necklace you are powerless. And your assistants can't stop me, I mean us!" continued Barry. He turned around and pointed to the wizard's assistants who were all now lying flat on the floor with goblins sat on their chests.

"Steve and Wally are now both locked up in cages and haven't a wand between them. The only people to escape were the Earth girl and an elf boy, and what can they do, they are just children," said Barry.

Unbeknown to Barry was the fact that as he was speaking, Isla was fast-approaching the temple riding high on the shoulders of a very angry troll, and Wally was just about to land outside on a fire-breathing buzzagon. Their plan to take over Atalan might not go as smoothly as they had first imagined.

Chapter 10

Isla could see the temple up ahead as Fizzbit closed in on their destination. He hadn't slowed down once and had covered the ground in no time at all, the journey not much more than a blur to Isla as Fizzbit had raced through Atalan with the speed of a giant cheetah.

As they neared the entrance to the temple, Isla could see Buzzby up ahead, about to land with his three passengers. How Fizzbit had managed to get there only slightly after a creature that could fly, Isla didn't know. It was just one of the many mysteries that baffled her about this wonderful place.

Fizzbit came to a stop and gently lifted Isla off his shoulders and placed her on the ground. After his sprint through Atalan, he wasn't even breathing heavy, not a drop of sweat or a cramped muscle in sight. It was a very different picture compared to when her dad would return from his weekly two mile jog, thought Isla. This would always finish with him red-faced, panting for breath and complaining of either a pulled muscle, stitch or both!

Isla walked over to Wally who had climbed down from off Buzzby and was now surveying the scene in front of him while stroking his beard.

"So, what's the plan?" asked Isla.

"Well, I have a horrible feeling Barry has beaten us to it," replied Wally.

"What makes you think that?" asked Isla.

"There are normally wizard's assistants guarding the front entrance, and there doesn't appear to be any around," said Wally.

As Wally spoke, Isla looked around and realised the wizard was right. The last time she had been here with Steve, they had been stopped on their arrival by Matilda and Noel. Now there appeared to be nobody about.

"So, what do we do now?" said Isla.

"We need to get into the temple and see what is going on. We will just need to move very carefully. Sophie, it might be a good idea to leave Buzzby by the front door. That way if anyone does arrive while we are inside, then they won't be able to come in and sneak up on us from behind," said Wally.

Sophie smiled and nodded.

"Ok then, follow me," said Wally.

The wizard led the way down the cobbled path and up the steps to the front door. Isla followed closely behind along with Fizzbit and Benji while Sophie brought up the rear along with Buzzby who she led by his reins. When they reached the open double doors, Sophie tied Buzzby' s reins to one of the large door handles and whispered something in his ear. She gave him an affectionate pat, and the giant buzzagon laid down across the doorway and became the largest and scariest looking guard dog that Isla had ever seen!

Once Wally was happy that no one could creep up on them from behind, he led the way through the hall and down the corridor towards the throne room. Luckily for Fizzbit, the doorways in the temple were big and the ceilings high, and apart from having to duck his head slightly, he could move around without too much difficulty.

Wally moved down the corridor slowly, scanning for intruders as he went. He has obviously been to the temple before, thought Isla, as he seemed to know his way to the throne room.

He came to a stop by one of the cabinets on the wall that contained wands and staffs and beckoned Fizzbit over to him.

"I really could do with a wand. Any chance you can help me, big guy?" Wally asked Fizzbit.

Fizzbit smiled and nodded, and with a slight nudge of his elbow, the cabinet's glass front shattered into tiny pieces.

"Thank you," said Wally.

The wizard scanned the contents of the now open cabinet before finally deciding on which wand he wanted. He carefully removed one and held it in his hands as if he was weighing it.

"Ah, the Maxi Wand 3000 GTI; this is the wand of all wands. It can fire 60 lightning bolts in under 10 seconds and is as light as a feather. It's been voted the must have wizard accessory for the last 3 years in Top Wand magazine," said Wally with a smile. It sounded to Isla as if he was reviewing a car, much like on the television programme her dad liked to watch. Come to think of it, one of the presenters on there was called Wally, or at least that's what her dad called him.

Wally waved the wand around a few times as if he was conducting an orchestra, and once he was satisfied with his new toy, he carried on.

The group continued down the corridor. Each time they came to one of the doors that led off it, Wally would signal them to stop before trying the handle. Each door was locked except for the one to the gym. As Wally slowly opened it, Isla peered her head inside, hoping to find the chief high wizard in there finishing off her workout. Unfortunately, the room was empty except for the large selection of scary looking machines inside, which Isla didn't have a clue what they were for apart from possibly causing pain of some type.

Finally, they reached the throne room, and Wally placed his ear against the door and listened carefully. He could hear hushed voices coming from the other side.

"What can you hear?" whispered Isla.

"Sounds to me like goblins," said Wally as he stepped back away from the door. "Time to see what this GTI can really do," he said, pointing his wand towards the centre of the door.

"What are you going to do?" asked Isla.

"I am going to cast a spell that will distraught the matter in front of me, creating a shift in light particles and causing a transparent effect," said Wally.

Isla and the others looked at him blankly.

"Basically, I'm going to make the door see-through so we can see what's on the other side."

"Ah, I see," said Isla, nodding.

Wally steadied his grip on the wand and cleared his throat before casting the spell.

"Before we enter, we need to see through the door and see if it's safe for us to explore."

The wand started to shake, and the tip of it began to shine very brightly as if something magical was about to happen. Moments later, there was a tiny puff of smoke followed by nothing. The door to the throne room was still solid wood and anything but see-through.

"I seem to be a bit rusty with that particular spell. I will try plan B instead," said Wally.

"And what is plan B?" asked Isla, hoping it would be an invisibility spell or a spell to give them all superpowers.

Instead, Wally carefully tried the handle to the throne room and the door opened. Once the door was slightly ajar, Wally peered through the small gap. He could see the goblins, who were stood on the red carpet. On the floor next to them were the wizard's assistants. They were sat crossed-legged with their hands behind their backs. Their wrists were tied but not with rope or tape but by what appeared to be some kind of electrical handcuffs which sparked and crackled with energy.

Over to the right of the room was the chief high wizard who was being held prisoner in a giant sphere of light, and overlooking all this was Ivana, who was sat on the throne with her staff propped up against it. Steve's rucksack lay on the floor by her feet. She had her arms crossed and a wicked smile on her face.

"What can you see?" whispered Isla.

"Take a look for yourself," said Wally as he moved away from the door so that Isla could see.

Once Isla had taken a look, she turned back to Wally.

"What's happened to the assistants and the chief?" asked Isla.

"They've been captured," answered Wally.

How Isla had missed Wally's sarcastic ways.

"I know they've been captured. I meant what are those things around the assistants' wrists, and what is that huge ball of light the chief is stood in?" said Isla.

The sphere that the chief was stood inside reminded Isla of a giant hamster ball, and the sort of thing they had at the hotel on her last family holiday abroad, which were used to run across the outdoor pool.

"Oh, I see. Well the assistants are being held by electrical bands. They hold the hands together, and if you try and move, you are given a nasty electric shock. The chief high wizard is inside an energy sphere which is basically like a force field. When you are inside one, they take away all your magical powers," said Wally.

"And can you free them?" asked Isla hopefully.

"Not with this wand, unfortunately. I mean, it's pretty good, but only the golden wand has the power to undo that kind of magic," said Wally with a sigh.

"Where is the golden wand?" asked Isla. She peered back through the gap in the door to try and spot it, but it was nowhere in sight.

"I can't see the golden wand or Barry, which is a bit of a worry," said Wally looking a little concerned.

"Where do you think Barry is?" asked Isla.

"I dread to think."

"So, now what?" asked Isla. She was hoping that Wally might have some amazing plan up his wizard's sleeve.

"We need to somehow take out the goblins and get Ivana's staff. If we can get hold of that, then we might have a chance of defeating her," said Wally.

"Leave the goblins to me," whispered Fizzbit. While his voice was soft and gentle, his face said otherwise. He still had a bone to pick with the goblins for making him do their dirty work, and he was ready to get his hands on them and teach them a lesson.

"Can you manage that many by yourself?" asked Wally.

Fizzbit made a fist with his right hand and placed it into the palm of his left hand before smiling and nodding.

"Ok well, if Fizzbit can take care of the goblins then that just leaves Ivana. If you three can distract her somehow, then maybe I can sneak in and grab the staff," Wally said to Isla, Benji and Sophie.

"I could do my conkaburrow impression again," said Benji.

"I'm not sure that will work this time," replied Sophie.

"Have you any suggestions?" Isla asked Wally.

"If you can get in there and draw her attention to the left-hand side of the room away from the sphere that would be great. I will then sneak in and around the back of the sphere, and hopefully, I will be able to get behind the throne without getting seen. From there, I will try and disarm her and take away the staff," said Wally.

"It all sounds a little dangerous to me," said Benji who by now was looking a little worried.

"We need to do this so that we can free your family and so that I can get back home to mine as well. We need to be brave one more time," said Isla.

Benji looked at her and then nodded.

"You're right, Isla, my people are counting on me. Let's do this," said Benji as he punched the air.

"Just be very careful. Who knows what powers Ivana can summon up with that staff and what she is capable of doing. Just be on your toes and stay alert," warned Wally.

Isla and her two newfound friends nodded before they went and stood behind Fizzbit who was all ready to charge the door.

"Ok, good luck, everybody. Fizzbit, when you're ready, you know what to do," said Wally.

Fizzbit nodded before placing his hands onto the door. He gave it one almighty push, almost sending it off its hinges, and then charged into the room, straight towards the unsuspecting goblins.

Chapter 11

Before the goblins had chance to react, Fizzbit ran into them. With his head down, the giant troll shoulder charged the group and sent them flying. Goblins went tumbling; they hit the ground and skidded across the bright white floor. Others were knocked clean off their feet and flew into the air.

As soon as Fizzbit had burst through the door, Isla had followed with Sophie and Benji close behind her. Isla had done what Wally had said and had darted over towards the left-hand side of the room and away from the sphere that was currently holding the chief high wizard prisoner.

Isla was desperately trying to attract Ivana's attention and take it away from Fizzbit and, of course, Wally. She jumped up and down and waved her arms around. Benji joined in as well and started shouting at Ivana.

"Yo! Ivana, where did you get your black feather from? A raffle?!" yelled Benji, followed by, "I bet you can't even pull a rabbit out your hat with a bat!"

Isla had no idea what that even meant, but it seemed to make both Benji and Sophie chuckle.

Ivana's eyes darted between Fizzbit, who was still sending goblins flying, and the three other intruders who were now jumping around and making a nuisance of themselves.

"So, Earth girl, you have returned and brought some help with you. It will be of no use. You are no match for my powers," screamed Ivana.

She jumped up from out of the throne and grabbed her staff and pointed it towards Isla. The crystal glowed red before a bolt of energy came flying out the end of it and crackled through the air towards its intended target.

"Look out," cried Sophie.

Isla reacted and was able to sidestep the blast, and it flew over her shoulder and into the white wall behind. Isla turned around and saw a large burn mark where the red bolt had hit it. Whatever it was that was being fired at her, she certainly didn't want to get struck by one of them.

Ivana started to fire blast after blast towards Isla, Sophie and Benji. Luckily, all three of them were agile and nimble on their feet, and they were able to dodge, duck and evade the oncoming bolts of red hot energy. Blasts struck the walls, bounced off the floor and even hit the ceiling, turning the once all-white room into a charred and smoking mess.

She may have been a master of staffjitsu, but she was a terrible shot!

All the time this was going on, Fizzbit was still battling the goblins. They may have been a fighting race, but they were no match for the giant troll's strength and power, especially when this troll was very angry!

121

Fizzbit had two clinging off his legs, one hanging from his right arm, and one holding onto his back for dear life. A quick kick of each leg dislodged those two goblins and sent them hurtling through the air and crashing to the ground in a heap. A swipe of his right arm got rid of that goblin and sent him flying into the sphere, which he bounced off and landed in a crumpled mess on the floor.

Fizzbit then reached over his right shoulder with his left hand and plucked the goblin off his back and launched him skywards. All the time, Fizzbit had a big grin on his face. Payback was obviously fun!

The plan was working perfectly and while Ivana was distracted, Wally was able to creep into the room unnoticed. He darted over to the sphere and took cover behind it. The chief high wizard looked over to him and gave him a thumbs up from inside her force field prison. Wally gave her a thumbs up back and then put his finger to his mouth to signal for her to stay quiet and not give his hiding place away.

"You pesky kids, stand still so I can blast you!" shouted Ivana. She was getting more and more frustrated by the second as blast after blast missed her intended targets.

Benji raced over to the pool table and started throwing blue balls towards Ivana as well as any of the goblins who happened to get in his line of fire, and who hadn't already been flattened by Fizzbit!

As the balls whistled towards her though, Ivana would simply wave her staff and the balls would drop out of the air, as if hitting an invisible wall, and fall harmlessly to the floor.

Ivana fired another shot towards Benji who dropped to the ground behind the safety of the pool table. The red hot blast flew over his head and slammed into the arcade machine causing a large bang, followed by sparks and a cloud of smoke.

"Ahhh," screamed Ivana as she watched the arcade machine go up in flames.

In frustration, she slammed the bottom of her staff onto the floor which sent a shockwave through the room making the ground shake, as if a mini earthquake had struck. The vibrations knocked Isla and Sophie clean off their feet.

"Ha-ha now you can't dodge my energy blasts," laughed Ivana menacingly.

She raised her staff and pointed it towards Isla who was lying on the tiled floor closest to her. The crystal once again glowed before a blast of red hot energy was sent flying towards its prey. Isla watched in horror as the bolt crackled through the air directly towards her.

"Nooooo," shouted Fizzbit.

The giant troll shrugged off the last couple of goblins who were still trying to fight him and threw his body towards Isla. He managed to get his large frame between Isla and the blast of energy and took the full force of the impact, saving Isla in the process.

Fizzbit hit the white tiled floor with a thud, smoke rising from his chest from where the blast had hit him.

"FIZZBIT," screamed Isla.

She crawled over to her fallen friend who lay motionless on the cold floor. His eyes flickered, and his breathing was very shallow. His green chequered shirt was singed and a nasty-looking burn mark had formed on his chest where the energy bolt had struck him.

"Ha-ha, now it is your turn to feel my power, Earth girl," laughed Ivana.

Her staff was once again primed and ready and pointing directly at Isla. There seemed no way to avoid the inevitable blast that at any second was coming her way.

The crystal glowed red and crackled with energy but before Ivana had chance to fire, a lightning bolt struck the end of the staff and knocked it clean out of her hands.

Ivana spun around to see where the bolt had come from and there standing to her side was Wally, his arm outstretched holding a smoking wand.

"Where did you come from?" Ivana shouted at Wally.

Before the wizard had chance to answer, Ivana continued, "You think you can stop me? I don't even need my staff to defeat a pathetic wizard like you." Ivana clenched her fists and held up her hands, as if she was in a martial arts movie, and let out a terrifying scream.

While all this was going on, Isla was frantically trying to revive Fizzbit. She was shaking him and telling him to wake up, but it was to no avail. He remained lifeless on the floor. Tears filled up in Isla's eyes and started rolling down her cheeks. She looked over to Ivana who was now stood in her fighting pose, ready to unleash her staffjitsu on Wally.

Isla could feel the anger building up inside her at what Ivana had done to her friend. She jumped up from the floor and charged towards her. She leapt over a couple of prone goblins as she raced across the room towards her target.

She may not have known staffjitsu, or any other martial art for that matter, but Isla had played rugby at school. She jumped up onto the small platform that Ivana was stood on and tackled her. She took out her legs and knocked her clean off the platform and landed on top of her in a heap.

Ivana pushed Isla off her and flipped up onto her feet like an acrobat, leaving Isla lying on the floor holding her shoulder. It appeared that Isla may need some work on her tackling since she had come off worse.

"Now you will pay for your meddling. You will wish you had stayed on Earth," shouted Ivana.

She raised her right hand as if about to deliver a deadly karate chop.

"FREEZE!" shouted Wally.

In the confusion, he had managed to retrieve Ivana's staff from the floor. On his command of freeze, a blast of blue light from the staff's crystal had shot out hitting Ivana. She stood completely still, as if playing a game of musical statues, her arm still raised up poised to strike.

Isla lay motionless for a second, staring up at the seemingly frozen Ivana. When she was satisfied that the wizard's assistant wasn't capable of attacking, Isla sprang up onto her feet, still clutching her shoulder.

"Wally, we need to help Fizzbit, quickly," shouted Isla as she pointed over to her fallen friend who still hadn't moved.

Sophie and Benji had by now raced over to him and were desperately trying to bring him round but were having no luck.

Wally turned around and saw the giant troll lying in a heap on the floor.

"I need some kind of healing potion to save him," said Wally, looking worried.

Isla spied Steve's rucksack next to the throne and raced over to it. She rummaged through it until she had found what she was looking for. She pulled the fizzy drinks bottle out that Steve had filled up from the Wizards Waterfall. She remembered what he had said about it having healing powers.

"Can you use this? It's from the Wizards Waterfall. Steve said it can be used for healing." Isla was hopeful that this alone would be enough, and they didn't need lots of ingredients to make a spell to save Fizzbit.

Wally took the bottle from Isla and held it up in front of him.

"It might work. I just need a powerful enough spell now," said the wizard.

"Do you know one?" asked Isla. She was really starting to panic now.

The look that Wally gave her didn't fill her with confidence.

"Umm…" said Wally

"Splash the water on his wound and his face and then point the staff at him and repeat this spell," came the voice from within the energy sphere. It was the chief high wizard, and she was instructing Wally on exactly what to do.

Wally nodded and raced over to the patient. Fizzbit was in a bad way. His eyes were closed and it appeared as if he had stopped breathing completely.

Wally undid the bottle top and splashed some of the water onto Fizzbit's chest and then his face. Once he did that, he held the staff directly over the troll's chest and turned to face the chief, waiting for her next command.

"Now repeat these words after me," shouted the chief as loudly as she could so that she was heard through the force field which surrounded her.

'Healing potion which I give

The gift of life

To let you live'

Wally repeated the words carefully, and as the last word left his mouth, the crystal started to shine a bright green colour.

Isla could hardly watch; she was willing the spell to work.

As Wally held the staff over Fizzbit, a green flash shot out the end of it and engulfed the troll's entire body. For a few agonising seconds, nothing seemed to happen but then the light vanished and Fizzbit opened his eyes and very slowly sat up.

"FIZZBIT," shouted Isla as she raced over to him and threw her arms around him.

"What happened?" asked Fizzbit who looked a little shaken and confused.

"You saved my life. Again!" shouted Isla with a huge grin on her face.

While Isla, Sophie and Benji helped Fizzbit to his feet, Wally raced over to the chief's force field.

"Where has Barry gone?" asked Wally.

"He's taken my golden wand and necklace and has teleported off to Volcano Mountain where he plans on getting the Atalan stone. If he gets it and places it inside the necklace, then I'm afraid we are all doomed. He will have complete power over everyone and everything. You need to try and stop him," said the chief. Her face was still as white as her tracksuit.

"Let's teleport through the mirror and go kick his butt," said Isla who had come over and joined Wally by his side.

"I'm afraid without my golden wand the mirror is only good for checking your hair in. None of my other wands are synced to it," said the chief.

"The teleportation spell in Steve's bag," cried Isla.

She raced over to the rucksack and grabbed the bottle with the potion in it along with the guidebook to Atalan. She flicked through the pages of it, desperately trying to find a picture of the Volcano Mountain, but it appeared as if it wasn't a place tourists would want to visit!

"It's not in here," said a disappointed Isla.

"I will have to take Buzzby and fly there. Sophie can you take me?" asked Wally.

Sophie nodded although she looked a little nervous at the thought of flying to a mountain that had a volcano.

"You will need to be quick. The Atalan stone is buried under rocks on the mountain. Once a year when the sun's beam shines directly onto the rocks, the stone magically rises up out of the ground and becomes accessible for a short amount of time. Barry has done his homework because that is due to happen very soon," said the chief.

"Well, we better not waste any time then, let's go, Sophie," said Wally.

"I want to come too," said Isla.

"No, Isla, you have the teleportation spell that you need to get home. Use it now and get back to your family while you can. If Barry is successful in getting the Atalan stone, then you may be stranded here forever," said Wally.

"I can't just leave now not knowing what will happen to you all. You are my friends, and friends stick together. I came here to help you stop Barry, and I am not leaving until we've achieved that."

As Isla spoke, she looked at the bottle of teleportation spell that she still held in her hand. The thought of getting back to her family now was very tempting, but she couldn't just leave her friends behind to be potentially placed under Barry's spell. She had to try and help them.

"Well, if you are coming, then bring the teleportation spell with you, and if at any point it looks as though we can't stop Barry, then you use it, ok? Do you promise?" asked Wally.

Isla nodded.

"Do you promise?" said Wally again, in a stern voice.

"Yes, I promise," replied Isla.

She placed the potion back in the rucksack and threw the bag over her shoulders.

"Okay. We will take Buzzby and fly to Volcano Mountain. Fizzbit and Benji, you stay here and look after the chief. Don't worry about those, they won't bother you again," said Wally, pointing his staff towards each of the goblins who were still lying all over the white tiled floor. A quick blast of the freeze spell from the staff and they were all turned into statues just like Ivana.

"We have no time to lose. We need to get to Volcano Mountain as quickly as possible before Barry gets that stone," said Wally urgently.

After quick farewells were said all around, Wally led the way out of the throne room and raced back down the corridor with Isla and Sophie following closely behind.

They soon reached the front door where they found Buzzby lying in the same spot as they had left him. It looked like he hadn't moved a muscle and appeared to be fast asleep.

Sophie grabbed his reins and gave them a gentle tug and a tickle under his neck which had the desired effect. Buzzby opened his eyes and lifted his large body off the floor and sat up letting out a yawn.

"Hop on, everyone," said Sophie.

Once Wally and Isla were safely aboard, Sophie jumped onto the front seat and gave the command for Buzzby to fly. A couple of flaps of his giant wings and he was up into the air and heading towards Volcano Mountain at lightning speed.

Chapter 12

Buzzby rocketed through the air and high up into the clouds while Sophie manned the reins and coaxed him to go faster and faster. Wally gave directions from his seat in the middle while Isla held on once again for dear life at the back.

If she thought her last buzzagon ride was scary, then she had been very much mistaken. That now seemed tame in comparison to this as they hurtled over the Atalan landscape at what felt like 100 miles an hour.

Soon, all Isla could see was the whiteness of the clouds as they climbed higher and higher. How could Wally possibly know where they were heading, she thought? Isla started to worry that maybe he didn't!

The next moment, Wally called out to Sophie that they needed to start heading down. She pulled the reins slightly, and Buzzby immediately dipped his head and started his descent.

They flew through the clouds at such a speed that Isla could feel her cheeks vibrating as well as her stomach churn. She was very relieved that she hadn't eaten dinner!

The whiteness was quickly replaced by a mass of grey as they plummeted towards a rocky mountain top. Isla was convinced that they were going to smash straight into it, but at the last second, Sophie tugged on the reins, and Buzzby pulled up, skimming across the jagged rocks below.

As they flew low over the mountain top, Isla could see a large crater up ahead that was overflowing with a dark red liquid. As it spilled out over the top of the crater, it sent up ash and thick smoke, and as the liquid hit the rocky surroundings, it singed the ground beneath.

"Lava," said Isla, mainly to herself. This must be Volcano Mountain, she hoped.

"Look," shouted Sophie, pointing ahead.

Stood on the other side of the crater was Barry. He had his back to them, and it appeared that he somehow hadn't noticed the arrival of a large buzzagon. He was stood by a boulder towards the edge of the mountain and was looking up into the sky. The sun was almost directly above him and at any moment, where he was standing would be thrown into glorious sunlight.

"We need to stop him. Only one thing for it, give him a blast of Buzzby flame," shouted Wally.

Sophie nodded, but before she had chance to give the command, Barry turned around to face them, grinning from ear to ear.

He was holding the golden wand in his right hand and had the chief's necklace hanging from around his neck. He raised the wand and aimed it at the crater.

The next second, a blast of lava was sent skywards, hauling ash and molten rock everywhere.

Sophie quickly took evasive action and pulled hard on Buzzby' s reins which caused the buzzagon to sharply bank right.

The sudden change of direction took Isla and Wally by surprise, and they both lost their grip on the saddle. They slipped off their seats and plummeted to the ground below.

"Uff," cried Isla as she hit the deck with a thud. Thankfully, she landed on her back and the large rucksack she was wearing took some of the impact.

"Ow," shouted Wally as he hit the ground just as hard. Ivana's staff that he had been carrying was knocked clean out of his hand and clattered over the rocks.

Luckily, Buzzby had been flying low over the mountain, so they didn't have far to fall. The pair also managed to avoid falling into the lava although their landing was far from soft! The rocks were sharp and jagged and very hot. Not boiling like the lava-covered ground but far from pleasant. It reminded Isla of walking on very hot sand without her shoes on.

Isla lay on her back trying to catch her breath after having the wind knocked out of her. She watched Sophie expertly steer Buzzby back around and head towards Barry for a second attempt at an attack. She had been so focused on avoiding the eruption that she hadn't even noticed that Wally and Isla were no longer sat behind her.

Barry though had watched the buzzagon' s every move and as the large creature circled back around, he was already ready and waiting with his arm outstretched and the wand pointing towards its intended target.

Once again, before Sophie even had the chance to give the command to send a fireball hurtling towards her target, Barry beat her to it. A flash of blue light erupted out of his wand and crackled through the air, hitting Buzzby directly on the nose and causing him and Sophie to be frozen in mid-air.

It looked like the giant buzzagon was suspended in the air from invisible wires, much like an exhibit in a museum. The smallest hint of a flame protruded from his mouth before it had been stopped in its tracks.

Barry then turned his attention back around towards Wally and Isla. He waved his wand towards his rival wizard as if he was beckoning Wally over. Ivana's staff that was lying nearby magically lifted off the floor and went soaring through the sky, over the crater before landing at Barry's feet. He placed his right foot on the staff, held his hands up in celebration, and smiled as if he had just captured some kind of prized animal.

"Did you really think you could stop me, Wally, with a tame buzzagon, a Bushwhacker and the Earth girl? If the chief high wizard was no match for me, then what chance did a washed up wizard like you have?" as Barry finished his sentence he let out an evil laugh.

He turned back to face the boulder which had now been completely drenched in sunlight and raised his arms up high.

"This is the moment I've been waiting for. The Atalan stone will soon be mine, and I will have complete power over everything!" He let out another raucous laugh. He should be in a pantomime playing the villain, thought Isla as she watched on.

As the sun hit the boulder, the ground around it started to shake. Isla watched as the boulder completely split in half and out of the centre rose a beautiful stone. It glistened in the sunlight as rays of different colours of light bounced off its surface and lit up the mountain top like a rainbow.

"Isla, you need to go now. Get the teleportation spell out of the bag, and go home before it's too late," cried Wally.

He was trying to pull himself off the ground, but he was obviously in some discomfort from his fall off Buzzby. Every time Wally moved, he would wince in pain and slump back down onto his back.

Isla pulled the rucksack off her back and undid the zip. The bag was pretty badly misshapen after it had broken her fall, and she hoped that the bottle of portion was still intact.

As Isla opened the bag, she was relieved to see that the fizzy drinks bottle had survived the impact and hadn't spilt out all over the place. When she pulled the bottle out, she also dragged out a number of smoke bombs, bangers and stink bombs with it. They too hadn't broken and were still useable.

She looked down at this arsenal of joke shop goodies that were now lying by her side and then looked over towards Barry. He still had his back to her as he waited for the Atalan stone to raise fully out of the ground and into his grasp.

Maybe, just maybe, there was something she could do to stop him getting the stone and placing it inside the necklace. First, though, she would have to get across the mountain top to reach him, and since the path over to the other side was now covered in lava, this could prove very difficult.

After Barry had caused the small eruption, much of the mountain top was now under red hot liquid and covered in smouldering ash, although there were a number of large rocks that stuck up above the boiling lava that could possibly be used as steppingstones.

Isla looked at these rocks that hadn't been submerged by the lava and mentally worked out a path across the mountain over to where Barry was. It could be done, she thought, although it would be like playing the world's toughest game of 'The floor is lava!'

She loved playing that game at school, although the worst thing that could happen there would be you step foot on the playground and would have to be on the next go! In this game, one false move could result in being burnt alive.

Isla pulled herself off the ground. Apart from being winded, and a few scratches and scrapes on her arms, she appeared to be unscathed. She gathered up the stuff from the joke shop and stuffed it in her pocket.

Wally looked up at her from his position on the rocks.

"What are you doing?" he hissed.

"Playing the floor is lava!" shouted Isla as she darted past him.

She hopped onto the nearest rock to her and steadied herself. To get around the crater and over to the other side and onto safe ground, she would need to follow a path over about ten rocks. She would need to move very, very carefully but also quickly, as by now the Atalan stone was completely out of the ground.

Isla leapt across to the next rock and landed safely. She could feel the heat rising from the lava that flowed all around her, and the steam it was creating was starting to get into her eyes and make visibility very difficult. If only she had some of Wally's flying potion, she wished.

The next rock in front of her was a fair distance away and would require a big jump. She bent her knees and swung her arms, just like she had done for the standing long jump at her last school's sports day. She launched herself across the gap and made it onto the next rock, but as she landed, her foot slipped from under her.

Isla let out a shriek and dropped onto her knees, grabbing the edge of the rock with both hands. Her left foot dangled agonisingly close to the lava below.

She pulled her foot back onto the top of the rock and steadied herself before very slowly climbing back up to her feet. Her heart was racing and sweat was pouring off her, both from the exertion and the effects of the boiling lava.

Isla took a couple of deep breaths and composed herself. As she was doing this, she saw Barry lift the stone out of the ground and hold it aloft like a prized trophy. She had no time to lose.

"Come on, Isla, you can do this," she said urging herself on.

She looked at the remaining rocks in front of her that she needed to cover and made sure she knew the exact route to take, and then she was off.

She leapt from rock to rock, landing one foot on each as if she was doing the ninja assault course at her local trampoline park. She vaulted off the last rock and cleared the lava, landing safely on firmer ground just behind Barry.

He was too engrossed in admiring the Atalan stone to have noticed Isla's arrival. She pulled out the contents of her pocket and launched it all towards Barry.

Seconds later, there was a loud bang and a flash followed by a thick cloud of smoke. Moments later, the air was filled with the putrid smell of rotten fish.

The loud noise and the flash that went with it disorientated Barry for a second. The smoke got in his eyes and temporarily blinded him, and the horrible smell made him gag.

This was just enough of a distraction to give Isla time to grab Ivana's staff that was still lying on the floor. She lifted it up and pointed it straight towards a very confused looking Barry.

"Freeze," shouted Isla.

Nothing happened, no flash of blue light or anything else for that matter.

"FREEZE," Isla shouted again, even louder this time.

Barry wiped his eyes and smiled at Isla as the effect of the smoke bomb drifted away.

"It doesn't work unless you're a wizard. In your hands, it is nothing more than a shiny crystal on a stick! Let me show you what a real wizard can do," Barry pointed the golden wand at Isla and laughed.

The staff may not have any magical powers in Isla's hands, but it wasn't completely useless. Gripping it tightly in both hands, she swung it towards Barry as if swinging a rounder's bat. This time though she wasn't aiming for a ball, her target was the wand that was pointing straight at her.

The staff's crystal struck the end of the wand with so much force it knocked it clean out of Barry's right hand and sent it clattering to the ground.

"Why you little..." screamed Barry, but before he could complete his sentence, Isla had swung the staff once again, this time slamming it into his left arm.

"OUCH," screamed Barry.

The blow knocked the Atalan stone out of the wizard's grasp, and it flew out of his hand and over his head. Barry watched in sheer terror as the stone catapulted through the air before crashing down onto the rocks. It bounced and rolled over the ground before coming to a rest, teetering on the edge of the mountain.

"NOOOO!!" screamed Barry.

He turned away from Isla in an attempt to rescue the precious stone, but in doing so, he tripped on a rock and stumbled. His legs gave away from under him, and he fell headfirst towards the edge of the mountain.

Isla watched in horror as the wizard disappeared out of sight, seemingly plummeting to the abyss below.

"NO!" she screamed.

Isla raced over to the edge of the mountain, being careful not to trip herself. She looked down and thankfully saw Barry. He had managed to grab a protruding rock with his right hand and now was hanging on for dear life. Below him was a near vertical drop down to the ravine with nothing to break his fall apart from some very sharp looking rocks that stuck out of the mountainside.

Barry looked up from his precarious position with a look of sheer panic etched across his face. His fingers were starting to turn white as he struggled to hold onto the rock that was preventing him from falling.

Isla needed to act fast. She may not have liked Barry and what he was trying to do, but she still had to try and save him.

"Grab a hold of this," shouted Isla as she lowered the staff down towards Barry.

"I can't," cried the wizard.

"Yes, you can, use your left hand to grab the end," urged Isla.

Barry looked up towards the staff that was just above his head. He swung his left arm up towards it and grabbed it. As he did, the rock he had been holding onto with his right hand gave way.

"Whoa," screamed Barry.

"Agghh," shouted Isla as the weight of Barry grabbing the staff pulled her forwards and almost sent her flying over the edge.

Isla dug her feet into the ground and held on with all her might. Barry was heavy, and she didn't know if she could hold onto him.

She pulled as hard as she could, puffing and panting as she struggled to lift Barry to safety, like a fisherman struggling to bring in a mammoth catch.

Isla summoned all her strength and gave the staff a giant tug, falling backwards and landing hard on her bottom in the process. As she pulled, Barry appeared over the edge and onto the safety of the mountain top, where he collapsed onto the floor and laid there motionless.

Isla sat there for a moment, her bum sore from the fall and her arms burning from the struggle. Lying in front of her was the golden wand and the Atalan stone, which was still dangerously close to dropping off the side of the mountain.

Isla pulled herself up onto her feet and grabbed the wand and stuffed it into the waistband of her trousers. She didn't want Barry getting hold of it. She may have just saved his life, but who knew what he was capable of doing.

While she was doing this, the ground started to rumble and shake. The boulder that had opened up for the Atalan stone to rise up was now starting to close. Isla didn't have much time. She carefully stepped over to the edge of the mountain and scooped up the stone.

Holding it in her hands, she could see just how beautiful the stone was; like a clear cut diamond, it sparkled brightly. Isla carefully carried the precious stone over to the boulder and placed it back where it belonged.

She watched as the ground it sat on slowly lowered back down into the depths of the mountain, and the boulder closed and sealed itself back up, the two halves once again becoming one giant stone.

Isla looked up from the boulder and saw Wally. He was still on the opposite side of the crater but was now up on his feet. He smiled and gave Isla a thumbs up which she returned.

Barry, meanwhile, was starting to stir. He had pulled himself onto his knees. His body was shaking, and his face was as white as a sheet after his near death experience. He looked over to Isla.

"You saved my life," he stuttered. "But why, after everything I've done?"

"Because I'm kind, and that's what kind people do. We don't go around trying to take over the world and forcing people to do as they say," said Isla.

Barry hung his head in shame and looked down at the ground.

"You are right, and I am very sorry for what I have done. I owe you my life. What can I ever do to repay you?" Barry lifted his head and looked up at Isla. Tears filled his eyes.

"Well," said Isla "for a start, you can unfreeze my friend."

Chapter 13

Isla stood in the garden of the chief high wizard's temple, taking in the party that was now in full swing all around her.

After saving Barry from falling off Volcano Mountain, he had kept his word to Isla and had done what she had asked. He had unfrozen Sophie and Buzzby before casting a spell that had made the lava disappear back inside the crater from where it had come.

Once this had been done, Wally had used the teleportation spell and guidebook from within Steve's rucksack to transport Barry back to the temple. Isla had returned with Sophie and Buzzby, taking a much slower and gentler flight back to the temple than before.

On their return, Barry had released the chief high wizard from her energy sphere and had freed all the assistants. He lifted the spell off the elves who in turn released Steve from the makeshift cage that he had been locked in. Finally, all the goblins were sent back to their kingdom and placed under house arrest.

To celebrate everything returning to normal, the chief had decided to open up her temple to the whole of Atalan and throw an enormous garden party.

Everyone had turned up for it, and Isla was now watching the celebration unfold with a huge smile on her face.

Over on one side of the temple's massive garden was a 'friendly' game of kicksphere going on amongst the Unkerdunkies and the elves. Isla watched as Oliver tackled an elf for the Merrybell berry, laughing and joking as he did. Fartybubble stayed out of the way of the action, stood to one side of the pitch handing out refreshments and shouting encouragement.

In the centre of the garden was an Olympic-sized swimming pool that many of the partygoers had made their way into. Isla watched in amusement as Fizzbit appeared by the side of the pool in his swim shorts. He gave her a smile and a thumbs up before running and doing what can only be described as a bomb into the pool. As he hit the water, he sent a huge tidal wave up into the air, soaking everyone in the vicinity. He also catapulted a few of the elves, who had been swimming, out of the pool and back onto dry land!

A dance floor had been set up off to one side with a DJ booth suspended above it. The famous Bushwhacker DJ, Afrowhack, was banging out the tunes for those below. Isla watched as Benji busted some moves on the dance floor. He had been reunited with his family and was grinning from ear to ear as he did a very good impression of a robot.

Next to the dance floor was Sophie who tapped her foot along to the music while feeding Buzzby some delicious-looking fruit. He purred with happiness as many of the partygoers came over to stroke the gentle beast.

As Isla looked around the garden, she spotted Steve over towards the temple. He was in deep conversation with Matilda. Whatever he was saying was causing her to laugh and blush. It looked to Isla that Steve might be looking for wife number two, and if he did have any thoughts about returning to Earth, they now seemed long gone.

"She's thrown a good party, hasn't she?" said Wally as he appeared by Isla's side.

Isla nodded and smiled.

"Ah, refreshments," said Wally, as a waiter dressed in a white t-shirt and black trousers, walked over to them carrying a tray of drinks. The waiter looked very familiar.

"Would you two care for a drink?" said Barry as he held the tray up for Isla and Wally.

"Thank you, Barry," said Isla, taking a glass of something red from the tray.

"Yes, thank you," added Wally as he helped himself to a glass of a clear fizzy liquid.

Isla watched as Barry walked off to serve more partygoers.

"How long do you think the chief will keep Barry and Ivana under her spell and make them work for her?" asked Isla.

"I'm not sure, until they have learnt their lesson, I guess. Anyway, they both seem to enjoy their new roles," said Wally nodding over towards Ivana.

The former wizard's assistant was stood on the lawn entertaining a group of fairies and Bushwhackers with her magic. She was pulling hankies from her sleeve, making coins appear from their ears and turning them invisible. Her small audience was loving it.

"Yes, she seems happy," said Isla with a smile.

As Isla spoke, something small flew past her. At first, she thought it was a dragonfly, but as she looked closer she realised it was a tiny person with wings. They smiled and gave Isla a wave before flying off.

"What was that?" whispered Isla.

"Oh, that was just a Mistgiant," replied Wally.

"Oh," said Isla.

Just then, the chief high wizard appeared through a pair of large double doors, which came out of the back of the temple and onto a balcony that overlooked the entire garden. She waved her golden wand, and the party fell silent. The music stopped, the kicksphere game ended and even the splashing in the pool ceased.

"People of Atalan, can I have your attention please? First of all, can I thank you all for attending my little celebration? I have a few people I would like to give special thanks to, but I will keep it as short as possible so you can go back to enjoying the party. First of all, a big thank you to wizard Wally for discovering this plot and contacting Steve. You are a true asset to the Magic Cone," a loud cheer and a round of applause followed which made Wally blush. He looked over to Isla, and she gave him a wink.

"Next up, I would like to thank Steve for returning from Earth to help his friend and in his role in saving Atalan," another cheer and round of applause followed, although Steve didn't notice as he was still too busy chatting up Matilda!

The chief went on to thank Sophie and Buzzby, Benji and Fizzbit before she came to her last thank you.

"Finally, I would like to give a huge thank you to one of the bravest girls I know." As she spoke, the chief floated down from off the balcony, over the partygoers' heads before gracefully landing in front of Isla.

"Isla, you risked your chance to return home to your family to help keep Atalan a safe place. Without you, who knows what our future would hold. To show our gratitude, we would like to give you this gift." The chief clicked her fingers and Barry appeared carrying a present which he handed to Isla.

"Thank you," said Isla, blushing slightly.

She peeled open the wrapping paper to reveal a beautifully carved wooden wand and the newest edition of the Atalan guidebook.

"With this special wand and guidebook, it means you can teleport here anytime you wish and come and pay us a visit. We all hope you will stay in touch," said the chief.

Isla smiled and nodded. She looked out over the sea of faces all staring back at her. Oliver and Fartybubble waving, Fizzbit giving a thumbs up from the pool, Benji still dancing even though there was now no music. She had made so many friends in this wonderful place.

"Yes, of course, I will come back to Atalan as this is my second home," said Isla.

As she spoke, the biggest cheer of them all went up. The chief clicked her fingers, and the party kicked back into life. The music played, people danced and fireworks went off over the temple lighting up the Atalan sky.

Isla celebrated with her friends through the night until it was finally time for her to return home...for now at least.

Printed in Poland
by Amazon Fulfillment
Poland Sp. z o.o., Wrocław

64089415R00085